The Clay That Breathes

The Clay
That Breathes

by
Catherine Browder

Drawings by
Stephanie Torbert

Milkweed Editions

THE CLAY THAT BREATHES

©1991, text by Catherine Browder Morris
©1991, drawings by Stephanie Torbert
©1991, design by R. W. Scholes

Printed in the United States of America
Published by *Milkweed Editions*
Post Office Box 3226
Minneapolis, Minnesota 55403
Books may be ordered from the above address

95 94 93 92 91   6 5 4 3 2 1

Publication of this book is made possible by grant support from the Literature Program of the National Endowment for the Arts, the Arts Development Fund of United Arts, the Dayton Hudson Foundation for Daytons and Target Stores, the First Bank System Foundation, the General Mills Foundation, Jerome Foundation, the Star-Tribune/ Cowles Media Company, the Minnesota State Arts Board through an appropriation by the Minnesota Legislature, a McKnight Foundation Award administered by the Minnesota State Arts Board, the Northwest Area Foundation, and the support of generous individuals.

Library of Congress Cataloging-in-Publication Data

Browder, Catherine
    The clay that breathes : a novella and stories/
by Catherine Browder.
    p. cm.
    ISBN 0-915943-63-8 : $9.95
    I. Title.
PS3552.R6827C5   1991
813 .54 — dc20   90-26184
                                                                                       CIP

"The paper used in this publication meets the minimum requirements of American National Standard for Information Sciences — Permanence of Paper for Printed Library Materials, ANSI Z39.48-1984."

for my mother and father
and Randall,
with love

Acknowledgments

The author wishes to acknowledge the publication of several of the stories in this collection in the following publications: "The Altar," *Amelia/Cicada 9,* Vol. 3, No. 4 (1988); "Goodwill," *Prairie Schooner,* Winter 1989-1990; "Kites," *Japanophile*, Vol. 14, Winter 1988-1989; "Tigers," *American Fiction,* 3rd edition, ed. by Michael C. White (Birch Lane Press, 1990).

THE CLAY THAT BREATHES
A Novella and Stories

Six Stories

Six Stories

TIGERS

For the longest time no one knew much about Auntie Bohray's new friend. On Wednesday my older sister picked up some news at the City Market and phoned Ma immediately: Bohray's man was well-off. He drove a new American car, wore a gold necklace and watch and ring. He paid the utilities and her two children's school fees, not to mention all miscellaneous expenses. The man only had two children of his own to feed. Well, maybe three, since a new one was on the way.

Ma was thrilled. "See, Dara!" she told me. "I knew something was going on." The only grudging note was that the man wasn't one of us, but Vietnamese.

By the time Ma got around to telling my stepfather, the subject had been discussed from every angle, with a half-dozen friends. What she told Tom seemed a bit thinned out.

"Bohray not just widow anymore," Ma said, over supper. "No good live in Projects. Need friend. Now Bohray have friend. And bran' new microwave."

"Is that how you spent your day?" Tom said. "Gossiping about Bohray?"

("He's just jealous," Ma said later. "Men here, men there. Same-same.")

There wasn't any plot to keep Tom out. It was just the way of things, and Ma's Tarzan English. Out loud, I always called him Daddy, because Angela did. I was the only one of Ma's first family who still lived at home. In my school diary, I called him Tom and Tommy-boy and Mr. Potato Head.

"I go Saturday," Ma said. "See microwave."

"Sure," Tom said. "But I don't like you being in the Projects."

"Bohray she live there!"

"I know, and it's a shame. Somebody'll steal that microwave right out from under her nose."

Angela got out of her chair and pulled on Daddy Tom's sleeve. Angela wasn't more than five at the time. Tom just looked at her and melted. I called her the Mouse. Whenever she wanted something from him, she squeaked. She had round eyes, a puff of curly brown hair, pale skin like Tom's. Whatever Angela wanted, she got. Ma said that was natural, since Angela was his own true daughter and I was just a step. Funny word, I thought. Something you put your foot on, but he never did. Ma made sure I got my share.

"My two girls," he said sometimes, which made me feel I ought to like him better.

In my school calendar, I drew a bright blue star and wrote: "By this date, Tom will buy Ma her new oven." And if he didn't? Sulks and cries in Ma's makeshift English. Hot Khmer words that could knot us girls against him. Burnt bacon. Burnt rice. It wasn't as if Ma got everything she wished for. Tom kept the purse strings tight—counting out her grocery money every Thursday night. "Dara," she told me, "you have to learn when to fuss."

That Friday I crowded onto the bus with my friend Chantelle. Only three weeks left. Both of us were finishing up sixth grade, although I was old enough for eighth. "Small for sixth grade," someone at church said once, which made me mad. Mother was small too, and so was Angela The Mouse, even if Daddy Tom was her father.

I felt the summer months pull toward me like a wide and empty boat. I hoped I might fill them up by helping Tom with the animals in his clinic. Chantelle dragged me down the aisle until we reached a double seat halfway back. She plopped down and said, "Whew-ee!"

"Come summer, I'm goin' to the pool every single day," she said.

"Maybe I'll go to the pool too, if my stepdad takes me."

The bus lurched and stopped. The driver stood up, his dark glasses wrapped around his stern, black face. Most of the kids were still standing in the aisle, waving at their friends through the window.

"You kids, siddown!" he said. "You, back there. Put your butt on the seat. Tha's right. Right down *on the seat,* or we be sittin' here a long time!"

Boys in the back row started giggling. They rapped out a song, hands slapping against their legs and the backs of chairs.

> "Put your butt on the seat!
> Put your butt on the seat!
> If you want to get to heaven
> You put your butt on the seat!"

"I'm gonna buy me a hot pink swimsuit," Chantelle said. "And those pink plastic sandals."

"Why pink?" I asked.

"Pink's my number one color. Suits me."

It was Angela's color too.

"Blue suits me," I said. I'd been thinking about how much I'd like my bedroom walls and ceiling to be the color of a Kansas City sky. "I'm gonna have my stepdad paint my room bright blue," I said.

"He must be a nice man."

I turned my head away. Outside, groups of children chased and jumped and lined up for other buses.

"How come you don't talk about him more?" Chantelle asked. "Being as he's so nice?"

I shrugged. "Not always nice," I said. The bus pulled away, and I watched the city moving in: the brick and frame houses, fenced and unfenced, one right after the other, and none of them too tall.

"You don't talk about your real dad either," Chantelle said.

"I don't remember much."

The bus passed a block of shops that I liked to look at—Florine's Beauty Parlor that sold Redken, a pawn shop, a drug store with heavy

grille over all the windows and door, and on the corner, Speedy
Checks Cashed. I used to think that Speedy was a name. We passed
Troost Lake, so small, and someone always fishing, quiet and patient
as a tree.

"Girl, you listenin' to me?" Chantelle poked me in the arm.
"What're you gonna do this summer?"

I hadn't thought about it, only about the color of my room.

"I'm gonna watch 'Oprah' and 'All My Children'," Chantelle said.

"Me too." I didn't like TV, but Angela did. So did my married
sisters.

I looked out at the city. From inside the bus, it was like watching a
movie, on a life-size screen, everything within reach picked up by an
invisible eye—cars and fences and concrete.

I couldn't remember the things my mother missed: wet farm
ground with animals nearby, cabbage and fish and rice cooking in the
house, the yellow-green sky the wind brought before rain and the fresh
scent left behind. Dripping roofs and leaves. What I could still remember were the sights and sounds at Khao I Dang. And smells, like an
army marching up your nose. I met a boy there, older than myself.
He'd spent a year living in a hole in the ground. He said he could only
tell when it was safe to come up by how much sweat and blood and
gunpowder were hanging in the air.

The bus pulled over to the curb, red lights flashing. Chantelle gave
me a quick hug and bounced into the aisle. "You call me, y'hear?"

I watched her go. She was laughing and teasing a boy who lived
somewhere on her street. She was so excited, she forgot to turn and
wave.

Tom drove us over to Bohray's that weekend. He waited until Ma
and Angela and I were safe inside—Bohray waving from the door—before he drove away.

Bohray didn't care much for the Projects either, but it was cheap.
She used to say there weren't many decent places where a Cambodian
widow could live, without moving to California. Anyway, now she had
her friend.

"Think of all the widows he had to choose from," Bohray joked.

"But none so pretty," said Ma.

I would have said the same thing if I'd been allowed. Auntie Bohray was the most beautiful woman I knew, even if Ma said Bohray had put on weight in the seven years she'd lived here.

"Bohray has a nice face still, but now she's got an American bottom."

Bohray led us into the kitchen. Ma cried out, pleased and jealous, both at once. She opened the microwave door, closed it, opened it again, and felt the strange pebbled lining, the buttons.

Bohray took some cheese and bread and made a sandwich, put it in the oven, ran her fingers quickly over the numbers. In no time the cheese melted, seeping out the sides. The timer dinged and she gave the sandwich to Ma.

"But the bread's still white."

"You have to buy a special oven with a browner."

"When Tom buys me one, I'll make him get a browner. Next time you ask your friend for a new car."

A few weeks back, someone had smashed out Bohray's windshield, for the third time. I don't know why Ma thought a newer car would get better treatment.

Bohray laughed. "His wife's going to have a baby. I don't want to look greedy."

"He come here often?" Ma asked.

"Yes. His wife told him no more babies."

"You be careful too."

"I am. I got you-know-what from the clinic."

"Don't you want him too?"

"It's all right this way."

"But you're only a number two wife."

"It doesn't matter," Bohray said. "He's not so young, you know. I can tease him about younger men."

Ma laughed.

I was glad Angela was playing with Bohray's son in the front room. I liked it when I had them to myself. Bohray put on some rice. The sweet smell of it filled the kitchen and frosted up the windows. I drew a cat's face in the steam. Bohray thought she was being smart, but I knew what was "what." Chantelle told me.

"Not so good," Ma said. "You need a husband. Like me and Tom."

I watched Bohray move slowly around the kitchen, graceful as a dancer at the Royal Palace. Bohray could have her pick.

"You come with me to school," Ma said.

Bohray shook her head. "I've been."

Ma waited until the evening meal to tell Tom. She served up everything he liked: pot roast, potatoes, rice, carrots cooked to pulps that made me gag.

"So-so oven," Ma said. "Cheap model. Can't brown food."

If she had one—and maybe Santa would bring her one before Christmas—she wanted the kind that took away the whiteness of bread, the pinkness of meat.

"Be nice, huh?" Her voice trilled up like a bird. "Angela, she like too."

Ma wouldn't stop smiling. I had to cover my mouth to keep from laughing. Ma glared.

"What matter with you?"

"Auntie has new Nike shoes," Angela piped up. "Pink and white."

"With velcro straps," I shouted. I wasn't one to be left out.

Tom dug his fork into his roast, faced it like it was the only safe ground above the line of fire that came at him every night. There'd be hell to pay if Angela got new shoes and I didn't. He looked at Angela. I knew what he saw. He used to say the sound of her name took the chill off a room.

Tom said he didn't care one whit what they said about him at the VFW. Those old boys can come and show off their grandbabies all they want, he said, and he'd just pull Angela out of his watch pocket. "How old is Tom Mapes anyway?" they'd say when we'd passed on to another group at the Fourth of July picnic. Old men, all of them, pulling in their chins, hiding their waists under red-and-blue Hawaiian shirts. "A daughter, you say?"

And this Auntie business. He never understood it, complaining that Bohray was no more an aunt than the woman who came in every day to help him clean and feed the animals in the clinic. " 'Auntie,' " he huffed. "You people wanna turn everyone into family!"

It's true, we didn't know Bohray until we'd all met at the Westside Christian Church. Tom's church. New arrivals, all of us. Adopted and cared for, given blankets and canned corn and ham. Sort of like the animals in Tom's kennel. Tom had helped out himself, lowering the back seat of the station wagon, piling it high with cartons and old grocery bags, making the "mercy runs," he called them, from one run-down apartment building to another, in parts of the city where he wouldn't have sent either of his grown sons.

"More people wedged into three rooms than you could shake a stick at," he'd said. Folks with small children who had to walk up three narrow flights, kept warm by a single heater-stove in the central room.

"A dangerous thing!" he'd said.

Tom had been carrying a stack of blankets up just such a flight when he first met Ma. She was Vonn Touch then, and if she'd married him at home she'd never have had to change her name. Tom likes to tell the story on me, how I hid behind Ma, with eyes so serious they made his heart sink and swell, both at once. Of course, Ma didn't know any proper English then. Just a lot of single words that hung together as she spat them out, sounding like someone punching holes in paper. He always seemed proud of that fact, that what little she knew could cover so much space. I think that's what brought him back to her, again and again. The widow man, Ma had called him.

Ma was still going to school, and now she was bringing Angela. Not that it did much good. Tom would drop them off at nine and pick them up again at noon. Ma dolled up Angela in pink dresses and hair ribbons and little lacy socks that would have made any man forget he had a son thirty-eight.

"Good class. Good teacha," Ma said, and Tom laughed every time.

Ma brought her teacher bags of rice, Cambodian spring rolls, fish soup, cheese and butter and crackers that had been donated to the church, with the "sell by this date" stamp already expired.

School was the most sociable thing in Ma's life, outside the family. There were lots of other Cambodians for her to gossip with, Vietnamese with their noses stuck up in the air, Mexicans who laughed and hugged and talked all the time, and that nice Syrian lady who always wore a scarf. Ma talked with her every day on the phone, scolding and telling her how she should handle her sons and husband, how she had to act "more tough."

"You make boys help!" Ma said. "You do!"

When Tom found out, he almost lost his temper. "Vonn, honey, you can't tell other folks how to live!" I told Chantelle, imitating the drawly way he speaks. I thought it was funny, coming from Mr. All-American, Do-It-My-Way Tom.

Once, when her teacher was absent, Ma came home sad and droopy. "Poor teacher," she said without telling me a thing. Ma phoned her just before supper. Angela was watching T.V. I was in the kitchen, helping.

"Teacha? I am Vonn. I so sorry you Aunt die . . . When you come back?"

I listened through the pause, to Ma's tiny voice.

"She leave you everything? . . . Oh . . . I so sorry . . . Maybe her husband die and leave you everything."

Early Monday, after we'd gone to Bohray's, I heard bowls clanging in the kitchen. No one but Angela could sleep through that noise. The blender whirred. A metal spoon tinged against glass. Water ran in the sink, full blast. Tom's feet thumped down on the floor in the next room. I went in my pajamas and found Ma looking for the Pyrex cake pans.

"Bohray says no aluminum. Only glass."

Tom scuffed along the wood floor to the bathroom. I asked Ma what she was doing.

"Making a cake. I'm going to bake it in Bohray's microwave. You want to come?"

"I have school," I said.

"I'll write a note."

I shook my head and slumped into a chair. With only three weeks left, I wasn't about to miss a day. Ma brought boxes of cereal, milk, sugar to the table, brushed the hair out of my eyes.

"You come with me and Angela today. Daddy will drive us over."

"You're missing school too."

"Yes." She giggled. "I'm a bad girl."

The clock on the stove read 6:45. Ma picked up the bright yellow wall phone and punched the numbers.

"Teacha? I am Vonn. I wake you up? I no come to school today. Angela sick."

Tom left the bathroom. I ran in and shut the door. I thought Ma was being silly, calling up her teacher in the middle of the night. Telling a fib, just so she could go and play with Auntie Bohray.

I loved school. All the students in bright clothes and socks, the green chalkboards wide as walls. It made me sad to think about it ending. Chantelle wasn't sad at all.

"Dara? You there?" Ma called from the hall. "Dara! Enough time! Come out."

I left the magazine on the floor. I'd been careful. I'd replaced the cap on the toothpaste just the way Tom liked, and put the lid down on the toilet. So many fussy little ways of doing things. "You do what he says," Mom told us. "You do!"

On Saturdays Tom let me help him in the veterinary clinic. He liked my help—it was free—especially when Flora phoned in sick.

"She'll drop out of sight one day," he said. "Like a stone in water."

I helped him clean the cages, feed and hold the cats so they wouldn't feel so homesick. It was the animals I liked, but I let Tom think it was him.

He'd even had a young woman helping out, a vet student, full of ideas about how to lure the public and let them pay on a sliding scale.

"All I ever learned, Dara, was the essentials," he said. "Anatomy, diagnosis, surgery, treatment. Nowadays, they all want to run a business!"

Delores would put blue and pink bows on the animals after they'd had their flea baths and shots. She'd hand them over to the owners like birthday gifts. The older people loved it. After Delores left, I tied the bows.

What a peculiar world, Ma said to me, where pets, other than pigs, had the run of human feeling. Cats and poodles, standing in for babies. I knew what it was that got Ma all worked up.

I thought about asking Tom about his own family feeling. I'd write out the questions carefully in my school diary. *Do you ever think about your first wife? How often do you phone your sons, or do they phone you? Did you use to see them more often? Why doesn't your daughter call you more? How come she doesn't visit? How come she lives in Milwaukee, anyway?* There were other questions too, some that I was too afraid to write.

Tom's sons had children, all of them younger than me. I used to ask Ma how come they didn't come on over to eat, like my married sisters. American boys don't do that, she said. "Grow up, move away. Strange world!"

We did go over to their houses, once in a while. Ma chatted and smiled, and the wives chatted and smiled, but it seemed like someone or other was always skulking off into the kitchen. Angela got on with Tom's grandkids for about ten minutes. Then something would happen, and she'd come sit in Tom's lap, in a sulk. I'd sit at the kitchen table and color or read my book.

Just like Ma's wedding. My two older sisters were there with their families, along with Bohray and every other Cambodian Ma knew in Kansas City, wearing their best silk sarongs. There were records and songs, and a shortened-up Cambodian wedding ceremony, after the Christian one, which took place downstairs in the church gym. (Ma complained that we weren't allowed to have rice wine.) Tom's sons, their wives and children seemed to stand apart. His daughter didn't even come. Ma sniffed and said maybe they didn't like our Khmer looks and voices, but I don't think she was right. I saw the lonesome way they looked at their dad.

Flora phoned in one last time, to quit, like Tom predicted. Ever since Mrs. Murphy's dog had sunk its tiny teeth into Flora's index finger, she'd been touchy.

Tom told Ma she'd have to help, after Ma told him she wasn't going to allow me to, anymore. He softened the asking when he said, "It's a family business, you know. I was hoping you could learn the ropes."

"Learn ropes?" Ma said with a sneer. "You pay Dara? You pay me?"

"Not a matter of paying," he said, getting cranky. "It's a matter of helping out. The money all goes to the same place."

"What if I want buy Angela new shoes? Pretty dress?"

"Don't I give you everything you want?"

"Not enough allowance. I want toaster oven! Bohray have new toaster oven."

Tom struck the kitchen table with his fist and stomped out. Ma spent the afternoon in a huff. I'd told her I'd be glad to help. "Not your job," she said. "Tom's job."

She kept Tom guessing all day and night, right up to the following morning. I heard her banging in the kitchen around six, boiling rice, lining up the cereal for us girls, traveling in and out of languages without ever shifting gears. Tom sat down to his bacon and eggs, and Ma went to the phone.

"Teacha? I am Vonn. I wake you up?"

Ma pulled the long, coiled cord and wound it around her hand.

"I no come to school right now. I help Tom. Feed dogs."

The Saturday after my last day of school, I asked Ma if I could paint the bedroom Angela and I shared. Ask Tom, she said. I waited until I sensed a happy mood.

"Why, punkin, that's just fine by me."

I told him I wanted to pick out my own color. I knew the exact shade: Lucerne Blue. I'd seen it on a color tile at Sears. I shouldn't have asked at supper. I should have waited until I was alone with Tom. Supper was the time Angela pricked up her ears.

"I want pink!" she said and swung her shoulders back and forth.

"Pink's for sissies," I said. "Pink stinks. Nobody in their right mind wants pink, An-ge-laaa."

I felt bad, speaking out against my best friend's color. Angela always made me lose my head.

She wailed and pouted, saying all the silly things you expect of someone five. She huffed around the kitchen, little hands on little hips, went up to Ma, then began to work on Tom.

"Pink, pink, pink!"

I rolled up my drawing paper and chased her out of the kitchen, through the living room, and into our bedroom. I swatted. I poked. Angela screamed for Daddy Tom. You'd think she was being murdered.

"Girls! Girls! Cut it out," he called. He didn't move an inch.

Ma took the flyswatter and went after us both, Khmer words hitting us like salt. We both got our legs switched. She made us sit on our separate beds and hold our tongues.

"Dara always gets her way," Angela whispered.

"Angela's spoiled rotten," I hissed back.

"Half-half," Ma said. "Half pink. Half blue."

"And the ceiling?" I cried. "I want the ceiling blue too. You can't have a pink ceiling. You have to have a ceiling like the sky."

"Okay."

Angela began to cry. I opened my mouth, and Ma cut me off. "Enough, Dara," Ma said. "You too old."

Bohray called that summer, before I started middle school. She'd seen a movie and said Ma should go. "And Dara too."

I don't think Tom would have suggested it if Ma hadn't brought it up. We dropped Angela off at my sister Phyrun's.

Ma watched with total concentration, and I watched Ma when I didn't want to watch the screen.

When the theater grew bright, Ma picked up her sweater and handbag and headed for the exit.

"Okay movie," she said at Tom over her shoulder. "But not hard enough."

"Not hard enough!?" he said, once we were in the car. "How much harder can a person stand? All those empty fields of bones. Like the title!"

"Too soft," Ma said. "More killing. Much more."

He watched her as if she were some stranger who'd climbed in his car by mistake. A small woman with a sweet and wrinkled face. Nice smile, when she used it. "Brave and feisty as a pit bull," he bragged to his sons, although at home he didn't care much for either. Now he stared. The light changed and the car behind ours honked. He was quiet the rest of the way home.

Tom sat in the living room reading the evening paper while Ma bathed Angela. I heard Angela squeal, Ma talking, her Khmer voice rising and falling, warm and open as a bed.

Tom called me from the kitchen where I was drawing. He asked me to sit down with him a while. I sat in the rocker across from the sofa. He cleared his throat and looked down into his lap. "Your mother can only say a few things about what happened before you came here," he said. "You know . . . her English."

I began to rock.

"I know about the camp and how the Khmer Rouge would sometimes come at night. I know you lost your older brothers and your father and others. But I don't know how or why."

"You want me to say, don't you?"

You'd think I'd hit him with a stone, but then he smiled.

"I've got me a house full of second-guessers," he said. "My first wife, Edna, didn't say much. Not half as much as your mother. Edna couldn't guess a thing."

He leaned back in the sofa. I sat quietly rocking, staring at the floor.

"I might understand things better if you said a word or two."

A word or two. I heard words rolling back and forth as though what happened were a car wreck, a one-time thing.

"I wasn't any older than Angela," I said. "I don't remember much, except the camp. Not so nice, camp."

He knew about the camps. The church had told them all about it. I wondered what he meant by *all*.

The floor gave a little chirp whenever the rocker traveled over the loose board. My rocking grew fast, faster, faster, as though I wanted to make that old chair fly.

In my mind, the days melt into one day that never ends.

I hear voices, the rattle of feet and guns: a group of men pulling someone in short workpants and floppy shirt; the sun against us, blotting out the face. What we see is blurry, a farmer in a field, hands tied behind his back. Two men, one on each shoulder, lead him toward some distant trees. I see a different farmer coming toward us. We are in the garden, just beyond the house. Ma says to go inside. *Soldiers. Quick.*

Through cracks in the shuttered door I see a tall scarecrow of a man with a drooping eyelid raise a sickle. "This is what we do to traitors of the people," he says. His arm moves, bringing the blade down across my Uncle Sothea's neck. Sothea's head lolls to one side, falls, and rolls a foot into Ma's garden. Ma faints, and two other women drop to the ground to help.

A home at the edge of our village bursts into flames. I remember the fire and smoke and screams, more young people arriving, dressed in black pajamas or bulky camouflage pants. Some of them carry guns heavier than themselves. A boy looks at Ma and tells her that we'd one day come with them.

Where? she asks. And why?

Learn new ways, he says. Forget the past.

When they leave, she spits in the garden dirt. Toy soldiers! she says. With young, dead eyes. Forget the past? Forget Sothea or the father of her children?

My pictures fade, sinking down in shadows. Ma keeps sending us indoors. More people come, more child soldiers. They ask Nhouk to be the village head. An odd job for Nhouk, Ma says. Too mild-mannered. They ask Nhouk, Who is sympathetic? *Sympathetic? Who to? We are all alike.* And still they come, eating and drinking and shooting Nhouk's brood sow.

Your soldiers, their soldiers? They're all the same to us. For this, Nhouk is struck, hard, in the back.

The pictures begin to spin, a movie speeding up, hot and sticky colors exploding in my mind.

They take Nhouk's boy and tie him high up in a tree. *There still is no one,* he tells them, through his tears and the keening of his wife. I am there, holding my mother's skirt. After four days, they take the boy down. A limp rag. Nhouk touches his lips with water and bathes his face until a girl younger than my sisters grabs the boy away.

At sundown he goes back in the tree, the girl says. And at dusk we hear screams from a neighboring house.

I looked up. Tom was staring at me, his eyes and lips two narrow lines. The only sound was the chirp of the rocker against the floor. Chantelle used to push me in a swing as high as it would go. We're too old to swing much anyone.

"Uncle Sothea died," I said. "Killed. And Ma saw Pol Pot soldiers take my father away. So she dug the money out from under the water jug in the garden and took Phyrun and San and me . . . We left for Thailand. In the night."

Tom folded the paper slowly, back into its folds. He took off his reading glasses and rubbed his eyes.

It wasn't my place to tell.

Ma got Angela and me up early the next day. "Zoo today," she said. "Teacher called me Friday."

I threw back the covers and bounced up. Ma tickled Angela's feet. Angela play-whimpered, and Ma yanked the covers back.

"You no get up, you no go to zoo," she said in English.

Angela stretched and rolled to the top cover. Such a lazybones!

The bowls were ready at our places, the cereal lined up like train cars across the table.

"You want Kix?" Ma asked. Angela sulked, shook her head. "Frosted Flakes? Cheerios?" Angela pouted.

"Okay. I give you sticks instead."

Angela grabbed the nearest box and poured cereal into her bowl until it spilled over.

A large saucepan steamed on the stove. I smelled rice.

"Teacher says we'll have a picnic too. Everybody brings something. Angela, look up. We'll see the giraffe today. You like the giraffe."

Angela made a face.

"Okay. You stay home."

"I like the monkeys better," said Angela in her squeaky voice.

"I like the tigers," I said, and grinned.

"Tigers! Terrible animals!" said Ma. "Tigers come into villages at night. Steal babies!"

"Not here."

"Why d'you like tigers?"

"Because they eat babies like Angela."

"Talk nice!"

"Maybe we'll feed Angela to the tiger today," I teased.

Angela smacked the table with her spoon, squealed, pretended to cry.

"Maybe *you* won't go to the zoo," said Ma.

"Maybe tigers took father," I said.

Ma stopped, turned, and stood absolutely still.

"Why d'you say that?"

I shrugged and played with my cereal box.

"Yes," Ma said quietly. "Tigers. On two legs."

I looked up at her, but she was staring off into space.

"Daddy Tom asked me last night."

"I already told," Ma snapped. "They don't show that in the movie. They show guns and shouting and pushing and bones. They don't show how babies die slow. They don't show how Sothea lost his head."

"It's only a movie, Ma."

"Some movie. Too soft."

I took a box of Kix and poured it carefully into my bowl. Chantelle liked Kix.

"You want sugar?" Ma asked, her voice quiet and low. I shook my head.

Most of the students and their families had arrived by the time Tom dropped us off. Ma waved at Bohray, who was parking her car in the lot beside the school.

"So many new people," Ma said. "Where do they all come from?"

A yellow school bus, just like mine, stood parked across the street. I saw the driver leaning against the front grill. A black man with dark glasses. For a moment I thought he was our driver and I started to wave, until I looked close. He was shorter, heavier. I felt let down.

"Here," Ma said. "Take the bag."

Bohray's children were with her. Her daughter Rohn had brought a friend, a girl with pink cheeks and long hair the color of sand.

"I could have brought Chantelle," I whispered to Ma, angry.

"No friends. Only family. That's what Teacher said."

I pointed at the American girl holding Rohn's hand. Ma shrugged. "Bohray's business. Not yours."

I pushed away and went inside the school building. I sat down on the steps and watched the adults going up and down, everybody moving so fast through that thick August heat. I heard laughing on the top floor, the school floor. I recognized Ma's teacher, a tall woman, carrying down a cooler. "Hello, Dara. Where's your mother?" she asked.

"In front," I said. "With Bohray."

I followed her outside. Ma squealed and hugged her teacher, everyone talking at once.

Auntie said something, but I couldn't hear. There was a sudden burst of voices just behind. Khmer words turned to shouts, curses, screams. I turned, backed away from the entrance and stood behind Ma.

Two Cambodian people came out the front door, backwards. A short round woman in an orange-and-black sarong pushed a man with spiky hair and crushed khaki pants. People on the sidewalk froze in mid-step, lowering baskets and bags to the pavement. Heads appeared from the office window on the third floor.

The man pushed back. Ma whispered, "I know that man."

The shouting woman grabbed hold of the man's shirt and began to pull, the man swatting at her hands. When he tried to shake loose, the woman took a firmer hold, both hands pulling until the shirttail came free.

Ma ran up the sidewalk and pushed the man down. Both women were on him now, like cats on a bird. Feet kicked up, elbows stabbed the air, limbs moving so fast that no one dared to help. From behind the school bus, a third Cambodian woman screamed and ran across the street to the group struggling on the sidewalk. She tugged on the man's shoulder, trying to pull him to his feet, her own feet kicking out at Ma. I felt my body moving forward, then Bohray holding me back.

The heads in the upstairs window disappeared. Seconds later, four teachers burst out the door and fell on Ma and the other people in the street.

"Stop it! Stop it now!" someone yelled.

Ma shook loose and backed away. I saw Ma's teacher place a hand on her shoulder, ready to hang on tight. The man's shirt flapped open, one button gone, the buttonhole torn. His mouth hung open. His face looked so old.

Ma let loose a string of curses that singed our ears. Not one Cambodian moved. We stood there in a cluster, motionless and afraid. This is a dream, I told myself. A camp dream. A nightmare that would vanish in the sunlight. But the memory pushed up harder, the harder I pushed it down.

I could see the man's face now, the look of anger and fear and surprise. His wife stood flushed and small-eyed as a nursing sow, ready to trample anything that came too close.

One of the teachers, a man, began to speak, the words never stopping, his hands talking, talking. "Back up," said the hands. "Calm down, calm down." Bohray held tightly to Angela's hand.

I came and put my arms around Ma.

"Khmer Rouge," Ma told the teachers and pointed, her finger a gun. "He give away my neighbor. Maybe give away my brother. My husband."

The man shouted back in Khmer. "I gave no one away. They came. They took. Don't you remember my son? Don't you remember the tree?"

Ma's finger remained steady in the air until it trembled. Slowly she lowered her arm.

"I call Tom," she said to her teacher. "I go home now."

I felt such sadness, like a deep, dark hole. All her one-inch words, her short and jerky sentences. I wanted to cry out, "Hush, Ma. Let me speak."

Ma turned back slowly to the man and his wife, and spoke in a voice that shook. "May the Buddha protect you, Nhouk."

Ma sat on the curb, holding Angela. I waved at Auntie Bohray as the bus finally left. Angela whimpered.

"I want to go, too."

"Not today. Daddy will take us Sunday."

"Auntie's going," I said.

"But we aren't," Ma said.

"Everything works out for Auntie," I said. "And she's not even married."

"What do you mean?" said Ma.

"Nothing."

"You say something but mean nothing? Strange child. You want to ride in the same bus with those people?"

"I don't care about those people."

"You forget your father?"

"No. I remember. A little."

"Good. You keep that *little.*"

The light in my eyes turned pink and dim. I felt in them a stinging cold, as though all the winds of the world had come to blow them out. I turned my face away.

"I don't like to remember," I said. "When I try, my head hurts."

Ma took my hand and squeezed it.

"You like it here?" she asked softly, and I nodded.

"I didn't mean what I said about Auntie."

"I know. We're all just number two wives. No good being alone."

The station wagon turned the corner and stopped in front of us. Ma opened the front door, pulling Angela onto her lap. I got in back.

"What happened?" Tom asked. He sounded annoyed, like we'd somehow put him out.

"Angela sick," Ma said. Angela squealed.

"Fever," said Ma and clapped a hand over Angela's mouth. I fell across the back seat and stuffed my fingers in my mouth until the noise that wanted to come out—the laugh or cry—was gone.

"You all right back there?" Tom asked.

"She upset," said Ma. "Can't play with other kids. I say maybe you take us Sunday."

Ma smiled up at him and laughed. "I so sorry for girls. Sunday okay?"

"I don't know," he said. "If I can get away."

"Dara and me. We feed dogs Friday, Saturday, Sunday morning. Then we go."

I sat up quickly and pressed myself between the two front seats. "Can we take Chantelle? Please?"

As the car turned onto the avenue, I lay back down and watched the sky. A bright, clear blue sky. Without a single cloud. I imagined the sky covering me like a blanket, covering Chantelle wherever she might be. A blue this strong makes you forget about all the other skies that come and go, the brown and black and heavy red ones that can press you to the ground.

THE ALTAR

Before dinner on the day Mori arrived so unexpectedly, Grandmother Ishikawa stopped in front of Heitman's veranda, stirring the contents of a small bowl. A spotless white apron covered her kimono, sleeves and all, its scalloped hem reaching as far as her knees. The privileged uniform of grandmothers, Heitman thought. Whenever he saw one, he felt suddenly secure, as if someone had waved a white flag of truce in a hostile zone.

"Try this," she said, handing him the bowl. "Eat a little with your rice."

"Thanks." He sniffed the bowl. "What is it?"

"A secret." She smiled.

"You have too many secrets."

"I'll tell you someday," she said, then paused. "Heitman-san, the grocer at the Co-op said that Mori was coming up this weekend. He telephoned the Co-op and ordered some beer and *sake*. So . . . perhaps he'll arrive tomorrow after work. Quite a surprise."

She glanced into the old house that Heitman rented from Mori, the former villager. Heitman's flea-market kimonos lay in a heap. Record jackets piled up where they were last pulled from records. Ishikawa didn't understand. She liked Heitman. He wasn't at all what she'd expected. He even ran errands for her in his van. Unfortunately, it wasn't a new van, and she kept urging him to wash it. Still, he was a good neighbor, and she told him so. If only he would do something about his clothes, she kept telling him. And his books. Only in the kitchen, Heitman knew, did Ishikawa allow herself the luxury of disorder.

"I think his family will come too," she continued. "At least the grocer thought so . . . Eat well." She glanced anxiously into the house once more and left.

Not pleasant news, Heitman thought. He rolled over and stretched out on the pillows scattered over the veranda. Mori was a nuisance and becoming more of one with each visit. He was glad Grandmother Ishikawa had told him. When he first moved in a year ago, no one would tell him anything.

Back then, Mori would arrive, unannounced, about once a month, and Heitman would make a bed for him in the spare room. Built next to a spongy hill, the room never dried out; so he never used it. When the rental agreement was made, the two men decided the spare room would be Mori's whenever he visited. Heitman considered this a fair exchange for the low rent.

A few weeks ago, the entire Mori family had visited. Heitman found himself squeezed into an inside room where he could breathe only if he opened the doors to the kitchen. Mori's wife had insisted on this arrangement. It was also during that first family visit that Mori had railed over Heitman's bookcase.

"How can you put books—books!—in the family altar!" Mori fumed. "This is my ancestral home. My great-grandparents lived here. And you have put your things in their altar! How can I let you stay?"

Embarrassed, Heitman assured him that the books would be gone by the next visit. No insult was intended. In fact, if Mori-san would please look closely, he would see that the altar had been restored. Then Heitman asked his landlord if he had recently become an active Buddhist, asking a bit too earnestly, he knew, as one might ask a lapsed Catholic who had just been reunited with the Church. Did he intend to pray at the altar? Heitman had never before seen him pray. (In fact, he'd never seen Mori so much as open the altar doors.) It was an irresistible moment, and Heitman asked in a loud, false, ministerial whisper, "Have you just survived a crisis of faith?"

Mori left the room angrily. Heitman felt sure the wife had put him up to it. He'd seen her whisper to her husband, scolding him about Heitman. She was the one who'd screamed when she opened the closet door and found his clothes in heaps. Heitman had refrained from asking her what she was doing in the closet. To add insult to injury, one of their children sat on his stereo and cracked the cover.

"But I haven't got a wife," Heitman joked, hoping she would indulge him, the disorderly bachelor, and loosen up. Instead, she continued to march through the house, making unpleasant discoveries. Even though it was his ancestral home, only the business of the altar had been left to Mori.

So they were coming again, and the altar was still full of books.

Attached to a wall like an ornate bathroom cabinet, the altar was in shambles when Heitman moved in. The wood frame was split in several places. Gold leaf had peeled away. Even the door hinges were tight with neglect. Small metal candle holders, black with tarnish, turned out to be brass, as did a small Buddhist image that had fallen, forgotten, on its side. Carefully, tediously, he repaired the frame, although some of the filigree could never be replaced. It was a professional job, and he admired it for weeks, letting it stand open and empty. Later, with infinite care, he filled the altar shelves with two neat rows of books.

★

Soon after he'd arrived in Osaka, Heitman's study funds seemed to evaporate overnight. He took a job teaching "English conversation" to the exhausted businessmen of a large, prosperous firm. Teaching was bad enough, but for a year he'd lived in a series of small, dark rooms. His teaching ended for the summer, and he discovered he was flush. On an impulse he bought a van, secondhand, from a caterer who specialized in funeral parties. Throughout that first summer, he toured the nearby countryside until he found the farmhouse for rent, in the village of Himachi.

Mori's old house stood on the crest of a hill, facing the rice fields, with its back to the road. From the moment he moved in, he devoted himself to the house. Sometimes he'd walk back and forth across the kitchen, for no other reason than to enjoy the uneven texture of the dirt floor. He would open the delicate wood windows just to feel them glide along their runners. It was hard to imagine that a place so permeable was ever considered a home. Rustic idylls shape the dreams of visitors, he soon learned, not residents. He was the only one who took the footpaths through the bamboo-covered hills. The farmers, his neighbors, drove around in their mini-pickups.

He settled in. In front of the porch, he planted a small garden, with azalea and gardenia bushes on one side, vegetables on the other. A scavenger at heart, he reclaimed an old chair made of wood and canvas awning. No villager would own anything so shameful, but he was overcome by its potential. The first time he sat down, the chair broke in one spectacular crunch, its joints poking out like a kneeling camel. He used it anyway, placing it in the middle of the garden and draping his large frame over it. Then, wearing a straw hat he'd found in someone's garbage, he read for hours among his eggplants.

The first time Ishikawa found him reading in his garden, she shrieked. The old woman began to laugh, flapped her white apron up and down and returned home, still laughing. Heitman was never sure what this encounter had signified to his neighbor. All he knew was that she began visiting him more often, bringing over pickles and village remedies, discussing the children, the neighbors, even Mori, until he realized he was no longer excluded from the small and closely guarded news that nourished village life.

★

Heitman put Ishikawa's bowl of pickles beside him on the veranda. In a moment he would have to start the bath.

Ishikawa's grandson ran past him, yelling hello over his shoulder. A moment later the child walked back to the porch where Heitman sat cross-legged.

"Have you seen my cat?" the boy asked, leaning against the porch.

"Which one? There are so many." Heitman sometimes woke up to find a village cat relieving itself in his kitchen. Contemptuous of villagers and doors, cats were everywhere and belonged to no one.

"The orange one," said the boy. "Like a tiger."

"I see it from time to time. Is it yours?"

"Grandmother won't let me keep it in the house. But I feed him sometimes. He's a wild one!"

The boy ran off again towards home, stopping abruptly to examine a twisted scrap of metal that Heitman had found crammed in the small furnace of his bathhouse.

"What's this?" the boy asked and held up the scrap.

"I don't know."

"Nice, isn't it? Is it yours?"

"No. Please take it."

"Thanks!" At the kitchen door, the boy was stopped by his grandmother.

"What is this, Miki-kun?" she asked, pointing to the charred metal.

"It's a boat!"

"Now, Miki-kun, look how dirty it is. Let's leave it outside, shall we?"

"I can bring it in now, can't I?" he asked impatiently.

"What would your mother say? Not until it's clean."

"I want to bring it in now!" he screamed and stomped his foot.

"What if it touched something? Look. It might tear the screen. What would your mother say? Here! Look what she brought you from the market. Come in and see!" The metal was left outside, and the door closed behind them.

The small altar shuddered as Heitman stood up. He reached the altar in three long strides and opened the doors. He would have to put the books in the closet for the time being. He'd planned to build bookcases weeks ago. Now the lumber stood moldering in one damp corner of the kitchen. Everything took time here, except the rotting of wood.

All year long, he'd felt the leisurely pace of village life seep into the house. Only when he went into the city did he consider the possibility that he'd slowed down too much, that he was as out of step here as he had been wherever he lived. Yet the very nature of the farmhouse encouraged a life based on deliberate steps—the slow-burning stoves and slow-running water, the distance between one corner of the kitchen and another, between the house and the bath.

Heitman crossed the breezeway to the bathhouse. Water flowed out of an old, arching spigot and into a cast-iron tub. He'd always enjoyed the ritual of the bath, perhaps because the old tub was the only thing in his present life large enough to contain him. Ishikawa-san was sure he would perish without a wife, to pick up his clothes and fill his bath, but he'd surprised her.

Outside, Heitman shoved a short, thick log into the bath furnace and lit it with kindling. The bath would heat while he made supper, and afterward he would clear out the books. Later, when he finally checked the water, it was scalding. He hurriedly pulled out the hot log and dragged it out of the way of early evening traffic. Miki-kun and his little brother would be out again soon, making their mad, postprandial dash across his garden.

He had to laugh at himself. He was behaving like one of the local housewives, sharing recipes with Ishikawa and worrying about the children. His presence was somewhat taken for granted, and the value of the neighborhood had not plunged.

Even the auto mechanic at the end of the village didn't scowl anymore when he brought in the unreliable van. Now he complained if he suspected Heitman of going anywhere else. He asked Heitman about American cars, but Heitman didn't know anything about cars. Recently, the mechanic had begun pressing him to share cheap *sake*, which they drank from a cup that had touched more mouths than he cared to think about.

He learned from the mechanic that Mori had a habit of drinking and driving and running off the road.

"Mori's car won't last another winter," the mechanic said. And since Heitman had begun renting the place, Mori didn't bring his friends up for long, boisterous weekends.

"Doesn't bring his little girlfriends, either," the mechanic giggled. "Takes them to an inn up the mountains. Back there. Stops here for gas first." He squinted up at Heitman and stuck his head back under the hood of the van.

"I can keep a secret," he went on. "I give him a discount, and he remembers my family at New Year's."

"So why's he renting the house? To a *gaijin* too?"

"Who knows?" The mechanic shrugged. "Your yen is the same as mine. Maybe he just wants someone in it so it won't rot. Or be robbed."

Heitman laughed. There wasn't anything to rob. His stereo was his only valuable possession, and now the cover was cracked.

It was also the mechanic who later passed on the rumor that Mori wanted Heitman out of the farmhouse. Out for good. Puzzled, Heitman asked why. The mechanic shook his head and looked away.

"The wife probably but I don't know. That's all I heard."

Out? And go where? Back to the city? He no longer held a picture of the city in his mind. He brooded a while over this piece of news until it faded and he forgot.

The bath water was still too hot. He read lengthwise on the porch and waited for it to cool. *Shakuhachi* music played on the stereo. By sundown, the haze had lifted, and there would be a good moon after all. Then the low-rising moon was eclipsed by Ishikawa's square frame.

"Excuse me, Heitman-san. Did the boys come by?"

"No, I haven't seen them."

"Forgive me, but the books. Have you . . . ?"

"I was just going to do that."

"Yes . . . it would be wise."

They heard the boys' young mother call out from the kitchen door and the children answering from the road. Grandmother Ishikawa bid Heitman goodnight and moved swiftly, soundlessly around the house in search of the boys.

Goro Yamaguchi, the master, was performing on the record, and he turned the volume up. The sound of the flute fluttered through the house like a cloud of balsa moths, and he felt himself relax. If only he could play like that, learn the technique.

He looked up at the altar across the small room, proud of the repair job, proud of the movable hinges and the highly polished statues that supported his books. Even the repainted wood shone gold.

Ishikawa and her daughter reached the boys just as Mori was parking his car in the gravel behind the house. The car swung open and he lurched out. He was drunk. Ishikawa could smell it the instant he opened the door. She tried to stall him, smiling continuously, plying him with a steady stream of questions: How was his family? his work? his health? Behind them, music from Heitman's stereo soared up, filling the house. Had Heitman-san heard nothing? Not even her words?

She could delay Mori for only a moment longer. And as she talked, she knew with a sinking heart that Heitman—oh, foolish man!—had not moved an inch since she'd left him.

THE BEHOLDER'S EYE

For the third time in as many days, Jane Draper hears the back gate open and close ever so gently. She flings her book to the floor and moves quickly to the adjoining kitchen, where the view is better.

"She's back," Jane whispers to Richard, whose lean frame is arched with purpose over the tiny kitchen sink, which he is cleaning.

A tall, slim woman, presumably American, appears along the stone path beside the house.

"You know who she reminds me of?" says Jane. "Cyd Charisse."

Richard makes a dismissive noise—a rush of air, a voiceless harrumph that sounds, to Jane, like wind in a tree. Vigorously, Richard rubs a sponge against the faucet.

"Does she think this is a public path?" he says, without bothering to look up. "We should charge a toll."

Jane sits absolutely still as the woman passes the north bank of windows and disappears down the steep, fern-lined stone steps.

"The neighborhood is getting overrun, have you noticed?"

"So? We're foreigners too," Jane says.

"That's different. We've been here longer."

"Who do you suppose she is?"

Richard pulls the oven door open and begins to scrub. "La Belle Dame Sans Merci," he says in a mournful tone.

"That's hardly fair. You don't even know the poor girl."

"Neither do you. But in almost the same breath you've called her both a movie star and poor."

There is little point in arguing. She learned long ago that it isn't Richard's habit to be fair: all his inclinations are critical. Beauty, like other things, must be earned, deserved, and certainly not given at face value to an unknown *gaijin* who has thoughtlessly chosen their garden path as a short cut to the street.

"I wonder where she lives?" Jane asks.

"Far away, I hope."

Jane watches her housemate as he continues scouring the stove. A mutual friend believes that Richard Ivey is actually a rare species of bamboo, the kind that grows a foot overnight. He isn't a handsome man, although Jane has always found him distinguished. Perhaps because he looks so elegant in a kimono, once he's let out the hem. Richard's been in Japan longer than anyone else she knows, having been sent over to translate for a large international bank. In the months they have shared this house, she has discovered Richard's hidden flaw: he treats most of his compatriots as one might an outbreak of pox, strenuously avoiding contact in public places, especially the market. ("Just look at them, Jane. What a dreary, vagabond lot!") Jane wishes he would at least distinguish between the scholars and the Hare Krishnas.

Jane feels a kinship with the vagabonds, which she's never dared reveal. Their improvised lives remind her of her own. Retired from the Peace Corps, she was derailed here on her way home from Korea. She has no special plans, and no one in Ohio, except her mother, is waiting.

Meeting Richard was a stroke of luck. He was looking for a roommate, just when she was desperate for rooms. Richard told her that he had been renting, for three years, half of a Meiji-era house from a well-to-do woman in her fifties. "Mrs. Yomiyuri is a lovely woman," he said with his strange smile that Jane misinterpreted, at first, as a smirk. "But you have to understand her." (Since she has moved into the house, Jane's contacts with Mrs. Y. are brief and formal, although there is something about her that reminds Jane of a Japanese Maureen Stapleton.)

   Mrs. Yomiyuri and her doctor husband now live in a suburb of
Kobe, but her large Kyoto family home, overlooking the Higashi
Mountains, is always in demand. Mrs. Yomiyuri speaks at length about
her previous tenants: the Fulbright scholar, the Swedish surgeon, the
executives from Chrysler and Zenith. She is especially fond of Richard.
He pays attention to upkeep. He brings in jonquils, azaleas, sprigs of
cherry and budding plum, which he arranges in the ceremonial parlor
upstairs. Once a month, she comes to visit (to check up, Jane thinks),
staying in the walled-off section still reserved for family use. And every
August, during O-Bon, troops of Yomiyuris in somber kimonos fill the
upstairs parlor to watch the ritual fire on Mount Daimonji.
   Mrs. Yomiyuri gives Richard carte blanche to sublet to whomever
he chooses the extra six-mat room, now Jane's.

★

   Jane is reading in this spare room when she hears the back gate open
once again. Across the hall, Richard is stretched, yoga-style, across his
own *tatami*. Jane gains the stairs and tells Richard she's going to follow.
   "Why bother?" he groans from the floor.
   She cannot probe the reason, can only feel fascination's grip, as if
this solitary woman carries something vital with each step. Jane watches
the woman pass along the path beside the north windows, then disappear down the shaded steps. Jane leaves by way of the back door,
through the small kitchen, and out the wood gate to the same path the
other woman has taken. Jane waits at the top of the steps until she is
sure the other woman has reached the bottom, then quietly descends.
On the street ahead Jane sees the woman pass the small tofu shop, the
tobacconist, the Fuji film developer. At the corner the woman turns
right, toward the neighborhood market, and Jane follows.
   Jane keeps a respectable distance through the crowded block of stalls.
She buys chicken wings for dinner while the other woman, further front,
selects a radish. Outside, Jane buries her head in a bouquet of poppies as
the woman leaves. Although she cannot see her face, Jane is struck with
how the stranger seems to float. A liquid arrival and departure.
   Since it is unlikely they'll be introduced, Jane wonders why she's
being shy. This holding back is a puzzling thing, to feel so watchful and
aloof. Perhaps it is something in the congested Kyoto air. Jane believes

the natives accommodate nicely to the overcrowding, hiding themselves in language that makes everyone polite. Not so the resident
aliens, who observe each other looming like gargoyles above the compact local crowd, and run. Jane has been here long enough to apprehend the local view: an ordinary Western nose becomes a parrot's beak;
pale hair and skin house demons. But this dark-haired woman seems
oblivious to it all, innocent and uninitiated, and Jane watches her vanish
into the street.

　　Jane is eager to leave. The market offers such an abundance of
choices and sensory events that she must return home promptly after
each visit and nap. The large house soothes her with its curious blend
of East and West. The Western part downstairs consists of a living room
and eat-in kitchen, arranged across a hardwood floor. A plump low
chair and sofa fill one end. In the kitchen four uncomfortable ladderback chairs surround a small, formica-topped table. A square of faded
yellow linoleum protects the wood floor in front of the sink. They are
the only Americans of their acquaintance whose two-burner gas stove
includes a miniature oven, in which Richard bakes miniature loaves of
whole-grain bread. To enter the house properly—that is, through the
front and not the kitchen—one must slide open a double wooden door
that is as wide and heavy as a medieval gate. Jane now enters through
the side where she finds Richard, vase in hand.

　　"While you were out," Richard begins archly, "your cat destroyed
Dr. Yomiyuri's lilies. Water from the vase flooded the alcove. Fortunately, I heard the devastation just in time. My dear, Os has got to go."

　　Jane has been feeding cats since she arrived, although Richard generally does the naming. The only ones left are her beloved calico, Mrs.
Alving, and a single offspring born two weeks after Mrs. A. crawled out
from under the house. Unlike his mother, Oswald is a vast orange hair
ball, stalked by disaster. Richard finds him loathsome. If anything so
much as trembles, it's Ossie's fault.

★

　　Jane begins to see the woman at the bus stop. At first they only
nod, until after several weeks of nodding, the other woman speaks first
and introduces herself as Lucy Hill.

"I've seen you several times," says Lucy. "But I'm never sure whether people want to talk. It's the lack of privacy here, isn't it?"

She holds up an envelope with an address printed in English, and laughs—a gentle, wind-chime tinkle. "Tell me. Do you know how to find this place?" she asks. "I'm completely confused, and you always look like you know exactly where you're going."

Jane is delighted, charmed, and cannot for the moment find her tongue. She isn't used to being noticed, or more properly, she is un-aware of it when she is. Yes, she would be happy to help. Anything at all. Lucy asks if Jane is related to any Drapers in Tuscaloosa, where Lucy has family who are acquainted with Drapers, although Lucy is actually from Birmingham, where she doesn't know any Drapers at all. The bus comes, and Jane offers to guide Lucy since her own destination is not far off. It seems that Lucy lives only a half-mile from the Yomiyuri mansion, and before they part, she invites Jane to stop by.

★

Lucy meets her at the corner, fearful that Jane will lose her way. "It's temporary. On loan."

They pass a reeking communal *benjo* and enter the apartment, a single, extended room, one of several in a long, squat block. Every-where, the austerity of a student's life mingles with the odor from the urinal, and Jane hopes the original tenant will come back soon. It isn't worthy of Lucy.

The kettle is boiling, and Lucy arranges rice crackers on a plate. On the walls hang several pinups and a glossy poster of a couple locked in strenuous fornication. Jane stares.

"Awful, aren't they?" Lucy says. "I don't plan to be here very long, so I haven't done anything about them. I thought I might drape the walls with fabric and cover them up."

The subject of cloth brings her to a pile of remnants behind her door.

"My mare's nest. I pick them up at flea markets. Do you go to the flea markets? Kitano? You must come with me sometime. The bargains, Jane!"

Jane does, in fact, haunt the flea markets. Her monthly appearances at Toji have become a ritual. It is where she buys her spices, her cotton aprons and wooden *geta* and secondhand kimonos that comprise her

Christmas gifts home. Her infatuation with the open-air bazaar has dimmed some in recent months, with the influx of affluent Germans and talkative, arm-waving French. She's observed the inflated prices of kitchen knives, used garments, Arita pottery, real and imitation lacquer.

"I have such ideas for clothes and fashion," says Lucy. "I use odds and ends. I love Hanae Mori, don't you? I love the old stuff, too."

She pulls a length of silky, blue kimono sash from the heap and winds it around her waist.

"I would love to learn the Japanese methods of dyeing. I want to go to a silk factory and watch them weave the cloth—from start to finish. Oh, there's so much to do!"

From a neat stack, she shows Jane several squares of smooth silk cloth, several smaller squares of gold-and-white brocade—enough material perhaps to cover a pillow, a pincushion. Proudly she shows off her purchases, while exploring what it is she plans to do, might like to do, just as soon as the plan presents itself. Jane has forgotten why she's come, or why it is she stays, but it isn't for the cloth.

★

The women continue their visits back and forth. The original tenant never comes to reclaim his room, so Lucy stays.

It is Jane's turn to entertain, and on this occasion, Richard will join them. Jane looks forward to this introduction. She is convinced Lucy shares with Richard a common bond, a mutual innate refinement. They will strike the same chord in their keenness for beauty, their obvious appreciation of grace. It's something she's always felt she lacked, although she's not jealous of those who have it. She appreciates the gift, is even drawn to it, as she was drawn to Richard across a room crowded with lanky Westerners on the day he agreed to rent her the spare room. Not that Richard isn't tall himself, but he knows how to contain his length, move his arms, cross his legs. He has the same tranquil and suspended air she now sees in Lucy. Richard is sure to approve.

Throughout the party, Richard is well-behaved. He even contributes some of his date-nut bread and a jar of Bulgarian cherry jam that he stores in a secret cache. Richard keeps up such a steady, anecdotal patter that Jane could swear everyone is having a good time. She is unprepared for Richard's comment later that Lucy is not so much tranquil as inert.

It's true, Lucy did rattle on about her cloth, about cloth in general, without any sense of direction. But Jane is always caught up *(entangled,* Richard says) in other people's dreams. Now Richard is being lofty, instructive, muttering something about Lucy being one of those who ought to be avoided at all cost.

"But she's so lovely," Jane says in protest. "So earnest, don't you think?"

Richard begins to smooth things over, clearing tea things off the table.

"Jane, dear," he says finally. "She's one of those women who hasn't got a lick of sense and never will."

★

A cold tea pot rests on Lucy's table. Jane limits herself to one cup for fear of confronting her hostess's public *benjo*. Their activities together have expanded to include several museum outings, the flea markets, movies, and one interminable evening of *Noh*.

Lucy returns, as is her custom, to the heap of cloth behind the door. She arranges a bow across her shoulder, another at her knee. She seems to have forgotten Jane for the moment, and Jane wonders how long it's been since she herself played dress-up.

"Out of all this, Jane, I have to invent some new costume for the club. What do you think?"

Lucy has mentioned, in passing, her job as a hostess. Jane knows other women, more adventuresome than herself, who also work as hostesses in bars ranging from seedy to middle-class. "Clubbing," her friends call it, although she has never been sure whether they were referring to the work or the bar. All one has to do is sit and chat and flirt, or so she's been told. She has also been told that blondes are at a premium—should she wish to change the color of her hair. Jane is at once fascinated and repelled, and finally ashamed that her reaction may only be the product of "a bourgeois mind." She must try to be broadminded.

"I'd imagine it's easier to teach," Jane says. "Everybody teaches, and you don't even have to know how."

Lucy demurs. A room of students fills her with dread. She would find the responsibility of teaching too frightening. Jane, who has seldom

worked at anything else, cannot imagine such a fear. Lucy turns
abruptly, her face urgent with a new idea.

"Why don't you come with me some night. They're always looking for new girls. We're paid well, you know. Think of the money."

Yes, one could always use the money. Besides, her classes are in re-
cess, and she's been feeling bored. She will think of it as an opportunity,
a broadening experience, and so Jane agrees.

"What are you planning to wear?" asks Lucy.

Since she's only now agreed to come, Jane is slow to answer. Nothing grand. She owns one fancy blouse that she sometimes wears with an
all-purpose black skirt.

"Perhaps with one colorful accent," Lucy suggests. "A red scarf, or
a brooch."

Wistfully, Jane remembers the time when she did favor a certain
flamboyance: generous granny gowns, noisy bangles, yards of Indian
cotton layered with beads. Since her stint in Korea, she has lived along
simpler lines. She might consider her favorite pair of earrings, she tells
Lucy. Gold hoops.

"You're absolutely right. A simple, direct statement."

They finally devise a costume for Lucy that is expressive (as she
puts it), but not outrageous (as Jane puts it). She reminds Lucy that her
function at the club is to attract, not alarm.

★

On the designated night, they take a taxi to the club, one of many
along a block of midtown entertainments.

Lucy leads her down a hospitable little alley to a door above which
hangs a pink fluorescent sign. Beneath the Japanese characters are the
romanized words *Chez Veronique*. They descend a flight of stairs so dim
and narrow that Jane regrets she's come. Yet the space below is surprisingly attractive, cozy even, broken into alcoves and booths. Lucy ushers
her first to a small back room where several women of a certain age are
changing into matronly kimonos. Another, younger woman in a red
leather mini offers them green tea. Lucy whispers that the manageress
will call for them later. Around the waist of her pale green sheath (once
a remnant) Lucy attaches a black fringed scarf. In the inadequate light,
Jane thinks she resembles a moth.

"I'm so glad you've come," says Lucy in a breathy voice. "I'm never really sure what's going on. And you speak so well!"

They check their hair and makeup in Lucy's hand-held mirror. The dressing room has no mirror, Jane observes, except the eyes of other women.

"By the way," says Lucy. "If an immigration agent shows up, Mama-san will give us a sign, and we'll just slip away into the night."

The ebullient manageress appears, her body cruelly squeezed into a dark green cocktail dress. Jane wonders if this is Veronique. With what seems to Jane an un-Japanese flourish, the manageress escorts them to a table in the middle of the room. Around it sit five businessmen, well established in middle age. A quick appraisal of the club reveals few patrons under the age of thirty. An odd musical medley is being piped into the room: traditional Japanese folk songs, Big Bands, Sinatra. Lucy sits between two men in identical, and expensive, blue suits, one of whom is bald. Jane takes an offered seat across the table, between two others whose faces, for her, will remain an embarrassing blur. Another waitress, a child almost, arrives with small flasks of *sake,* porcelain cups, two Suntori whiskies, and colored water for the "girls."

Cheery introductions all around. Jane explains herself in Japanese and on behalf of Lucy. She is relieved that the formalities remain so neutral and unrevealing, until the hand of the man to Lucy's right disappears beneath the table. Jane feels the sea change swelling up from the floor. The man asks in a hard-edged English, devoid of articles, what the girls think of Japanese men. The men convulse in knee-slapping laughter, and Lucy offers up her sweet, oblivious smile.

Jane cannot remember her answer or even the drift of conversation. The evening becomes for her as smoky as the air above the table. Drinks and hands arrive and depart with increasing regularity, and she strains to listen, to keep her words afloat. She remembers stopping now and then, as though coming up for air, to lean toward Lucy and translate. (How on earth has Lucy managed so far?) She thinks she detects a territorial struggle between the men on either side of Lucy. There is little struggle over her, although the man on her right pats her arm and brags to the others about her Japanese. *("Jozu, ne!")* A sure sign, Jane thinks, that her speech is hilariously flawed. She thinks of Richard and

his impeccable verbs. He dazzles, he charms. He's fluent enough to tell
jokes. And Jane hears her own words lurch and rattle like loose freight.

Lucy's smile is as steady as the ten eyes upon her. Her movements,
when she does move, are slow and smooth. Jane wonders what it is
she's seeing here, besides lust. A pulse of longing and melancholia? The
delicate *wabi-sabi* of the unrequited?

Perhaps they are drawn to the perfect alignnment of Lucy's fea-
tures, from eyes to nose to chin. The prominent swell of breasts like the
crest of a fine white wave. The flawless, opalescent skin. Lucy's rich,
dark hair is cut in a smart cap, like Clara Bow's, where each and every
strand rests compatibly beside its neighbor. Jane imagines Lucy at night,
surrounded by organic hair salads, baby powder, Jean Naté, laboratory-
tested, scent-free lubricants that prevent her from drying out.

Jane wishes that she could appreciate and not compare. She would
prefer not to think about her own muddy hair with its uncontrollable
ringlets, or her freckled Midwestern face. She is a person whose buttons
pop, who forgets about unraveled cuffs and hems. She carries with her
an irrepressible energy that makes her feel out of place.

In the West, Jane is dimly aware, her nature does not go unrecog-
nized or unrewarded. In her present life, however, she fears it forms a
wall.

As the evening's tour draws to a merciful close, Jane finds herself
pitying the company men around the table, exiled from home, except
on Sundays. Jane feels the elemental sadness in the air and watches as
these five homesick men fall, besotted, for Lucy.

★

Kitchen lights are blazing when Jane returns home at midnight.
Richard, in his house *kimono,* greets her at the door.

"I don't believe you put yourself through that," he says. "Prepared
as I always am for the worst, I thought you might need some cheer."

The kettle is steaming. On the table he's arranged three kinds of
pastry and a spray of gladiolas. Jane sinks into a chair and allows Richard to pound the club out of her neck and back and shoulders.

"Richard, I'd gladly give one year of life to own an impressive
bosom."

"Lucy has one, I take it."

"She does. And it hasn't done her a bit of harm."

"Just remember. Large bosoms have a way of flattening out in the fullness of time."

He viciously thumbs a knot near her spine.

"Before you feel too comfortable," he adds. "I have a small report. Your cat Oswald attacked Mrs. Yomiyuri's pet cockatiel."

Jane moans, as much from the pressure of Richard's thumb as from his news.

"The dear lady, daft as a warm day in December, let the damn bird out of its cage. It flew straight out the window and into the azaleas. Your cat suddenly appeared. All it took was one pounce."

★

Jane has not seen Lucy since the night at the club, nor has Lucy made an effort to contact her. Each time Jane considers dropping in, something impedes the urge. There is a letter to write, shopping to do, a surprise visit from a fellow teacher—an amusing English girl (a vagabond) with hair as disorderly as Jane's. As her classes resume, Jane's attention is pleasantly diverted by a new teaching colleague, a young man from Illinois whose clear interest has sent her to an expensive hair salon.

When Richard sees her once exuberant hair now cut and shingled, he flings himself across the pint-sized sofa and covers his eyes with his hand.

"Good lord! Why? It looks like an artichoke."

Too proud to show that she is hurt, Jane flips the bottom fringy layer up and down.

" 'A change is as good as a rest,' " she says.

Jane's young man takes no notice of her hair, and Jane decides, after careful consultation in many mirrors, that this is just as well. Over the course of several weeks, his interest has run both hot and cold. She tells herself that too many years among his native corn may have limited his imagination. She decides his case is hopeless when he begins to dog the steps of a Japanese teacher named Miss Toi, a pert young woman of tiny proportions who is called, behind her back, "Kawaiiko-chan"— Miss Cutie.

Jane has often marveled how quiet Richard is about the details of his life. There was even a time, long ago, when Jane had thought he

might gravitate toward someone like Lucy, but this was before he'd
made his preferences known. Whoever may be the object of his
affection, if there is anyone, is never brought to the house.

Jane takes comfort in other friends. Her favorite is a former student
who treats her with uncommon warmth. Kimiko is short and plump and
covers her mouth when she laughs, which is often. She wasn't a gifted student, but a pleasant one, and now she often invites Jane to her home. Of
all the places Jane has been, the small room where Kimiko's mother enter-
tains is the most welcoming and serene. A puzzling fact, she thinks, since
the occasions are handled with something sweetly formal. Whenever she
visits, they usually sit on the floor, around a long, low cherry wood table,
drinking a variety of imported coffees and teas. She is learning how to
fold tiny paper lobsters, boxes, and cranes. Under their tutelage she arranges a flowering quince branch against a bed of moss. She is struck at
how comfortable these women are, speaking only with their hands.

She finds it odd, and vaguely troubling, that only in this simple
room can she think about the restfulness that has eluded her so long.
Something in the pell-mell nature of her daily life holds the thought at
bay. Only here does she consider how improvisation is not enough.

At home, Kimiko seldom uses English, and Jane's ragged Japanese
does much to break the ice. They laugh and correct her verbs. What
eloquent honorifics she learns! Even her intonation is improving. The
mother no longer calls her *Sensei* (a ponderous word, Jane thinks,
weighted with Oriental responsibility). Nowadays she is called, simply,
Jane-san.

Surely the soul of Japan resides here, inside the triangle formed by
the aproned mother, the rice cooker, and the teapot. It is Jane's most
treasured discovery, but Richard disagrees. The Japanese soul, he tells
her, is kept safe in a corporate vault.

★

Jane is swinging from a trolley strap. She pulls the rope for her stop
and sees Lucy coming toward her. As the white-gloved conductor shifts
the gear around its wheel, the streetcar sways and stops.

"I've been meaning and meaning to get in touch," Lucy says.
"There's something I must talk to you about."

The crowd disperses, and they make their way across the street.

"I've had the most horrible outbreak," Lucy says in a solemn voice. "I'm just beside myself. All I do is stay inside until it's time to go to the market or the Club. Then I cover my face with makeup and hope no one will notice. But they notice everything here, don't they? Every spot, stain, or lump. Last week, when I had my first attack, Mama-san noticed immediately. She asked if I was eating properly. She even gave me a tiny dab of money to buy oranges. For my skin, she said. Look!"

Lucy points to the corner of her mouth. Jane leans over to examine the disfiguring blemishes and sees three microscopic bumps, darker only by a shade than the surrounding flesh.

"Some mornings when I get up, it looks as if my face were blooming."

"Maybe it's the club," Jane says. "The stress. Night after night."

"You're probably right. I've been thinking about a little trip somewhere. To the countryside. Some resort somewhere. Just to get away. Oh, I don't know. I'll have to think about it."

Lucy seems eager to return to her closet of a room, and Jane leaves her with numerous motherly blessings: Stop fretting. Sleep eight hours. Come over any time.

But Lucy doesn't stop over, and Jane is for a time too busy to check in. When she does see Lucy, it is a quick glimpse of her on a departing bus. Jane stops by that evening. She finds Lucy reading in bed, looking unnaturally limp.

"Sunlight is what you need," Jane says in a cheery voice. "Activity."

Lucy readily agrees, confessing that she's even visited a doctor. Jane believes the remedy is a steady, daytime job, for Lucy has even lost her burning interest in cloth.

"I had a strange experience," Lucy says. Jane busies herself making tea.

"I met an interesting man at the club. He's some sort of upper-level manager with a import-export firm. He's been coming to the club to practice his English, and we've met a few times during the day. He talks a great deal about his family, and I mentioned that I'd love to meet them. Do you know that in all the months I've lived here, I've never once been invited to anyone's home?"

Jane feels her breath quicken. She thinks of Kimiko's house. The indulgent, nesting mother. The profound absence of men.

"But last week he invited me to dinner," Lucy says. "I was thrilled. I assumed I was going to his house. I arranged to meet him at the train station. I stopped ahead of time and picked up a package of wrapped fruit as a gift. He met me and was so gracious. We got in a taxi. Of course I didn't know where we were. I never do. We got out later at a building downtown and went upstairs to a very expensive-looking restaurant. French, it turned out.

"I asked him, 'Are we meeting your wife here?' He answered that unfortunately his wife had some urgent family business, and it was impossible for her to join us. She was terribly sorry. He hoped I would forgive her. I handed him the box of kiwi fruit, but he refused it emphatically, saying his wife would be too embarrassed. He was sure they had been expensive and said I should keep them to enjoy myself. I didn't know what to do, so I kept them. Later in the evening, over dessert, he brought out a small box and gave it to me, saying it was a sample of the products they exported. See . . . ?"

Lucy pulls out a chain hidden behind her collar, with a black pearl on one end. Synthetic, Jane thinks. Inexpensive.

"Then today," Lucy continues, "he invited me to the park. To take pictures of the flower beds. So I met him there, and he took pictures, mostly of me rather than the flowers. We went to a very lovely place for tea and cakes. *O-mochi,* he called them. Very traditional, he said. Then he asked if I would like to go to a hotel. He had one in mind. Around the corner. 'To play,' he said. I just stared at him. I was totally unprepared. All this time I thought it was for the English. What a fool I've been!"

There are tears in Lucy's eyes, and Jane hurriedly refills their cups.

" 'No,' I said. 'I have an appointment. So sorry.' And all that. Tell me, Jane. How can I possibly go back to work? He'll probably be there."

Jane withholds the first question that comes to mind: Why hadn't Lucy embrace the moment, thrown caution to the wind? Instead she suggests that Lucy take a few days off. A week. Explain that she's been ill.

Jane cannot help but notice the posters that still decorate the walls, and now she feels utterly confused. How can anyone so lovely, so accustomed to attention, be so awkward about arranging to her advantage the details of her life?

When she has listened and counseled as best she can, Jane makes her way home, exhausted. She finds Richard on the sofa, tie loosened, dressed in a three-piece suit. He's had a tiring business dinner, he explains. He and his Japanese associates were entertained by elderly *geishas* who sang, in wobbly voices, a repertoire of time-honored and tuneless songs.

"And what of you?" he asks.

Her head is made of iron, and she can barely shake it. She reports on Lucy, and he pours them both a brandy from an open bottle on the table.

"Listen. There's a nice young man in our office who wants to hire an English tutor. He can afford to pay well. Do you suppose old Luce would go for that?"

Jane hugs him, drinks the brandy, and asks for more.

"I do have one small report," he sniffs. "Your hideous cat Oswald laid waste to my garden. I just thought you ought to know. Sherman couldn't have done a better job in his March to the Sea."

★

Richard makes the arrangements. He will bring Yoshi, and Lucy will accompany Jane. They will rendezvous at a subdued little coffee shop famous for its classical records. Richard draws out elaborate directions, grows testy about the precise hour, instructs Jane to instruct Lucy in what to wear: no diaphanous costumes made up out of scraps.

"Something tasteful and Western."

They find the two men seated at a table in the back. When Yoshi turns to greet them, Jane feels herself grow dizzy. Here is a man of unrivaled beauty, elegant as Richard, but something more. Where Richard is lean, Yoshi is all muscle and tendon, an indigenous shape that comes from walking everywhere and playing tennis, from eating rice and pickles and fish.

Jane imagines Yoshi in kimono, stretched across casually-tossed cushions. She sees him acting in samurai films, running barefoot through rain-soaked alleys, his kimono whipping around bare taut legs, a sword deftly slicing through villains and rope. For a moment he even reminds her of that inscrutable and husky-throated heartthrob, Inspector Nomura, who moves each week through the saxophone-haunted streets of a popular television drama.

An incomparable host, Richard makes everyone feel cozy, in two languages. There is something a little calculated in his role, however, for he has hardly given Lucy a chance to speak. Her few words have been corralled and carefully lassoed. As Richard chats, Jane watches a cord of interest growing between the principals. Jane cannot take her eyes off Yoshi, but his are glued to her friend.

At home Richard views the silent specter drooping at the kitchen table and asks, "Are we all right?"

"Why didn't you save him for me?" Jane asks, glaring.

Richard covers his heart with his hand. His eyes flutter shut.

"Because he's simply not your type."

"And who is, pray tell?"

"That remains to be seen."

Jane allows the decent interval of one week to pass before making her way to Lucy's. Lucy is glad to see her, and explains, when asked, that Yoshi is "very nice." Jane is disappointed by this flat report. What is it that she's hoped for? To discover that Yoshi is a horror? A spoiled and petulant rogue?

"In fact, he was over last night," Lucy says. "I found him rather shy. Afterward I thought maybe he was embarrassed by all those dreadful pictures on the wall. You know, I don't even see them anymore."

★

Jane drops by several other times but finds no one at home. When she does see Lucy, she's returning from the market, her string bag full of cake and flowers. She drags Jane back to the room, which has been transformed. Folk-cloth curtains of delicate, irregular blues cover the windows above the sink. On the dresser are a group of wooden, hand-carved toys—animals of the zodiac. A small television stands in one corner. The walls have also changed. Gone are the fornicators and nudes, replaced by photographs of Lucy, flowers, children, birds in flight.

"Yoshi took them. He's splendid, isn't he? Look! He gave me this." She brings out a new Pentax camera. "He's taking me to Shikoku next weekend. A photographic trip. Isn't it exciting?"

Yes, Jane agrees in a small voice, it is all very exciting.

"I must get Yoshi to take your portrait. And Richard's too. He takes such good photos of people, don't you think?"

Jane makes her way home after a thorough and vanquishing discussion of Yoshi. She has no strength to use against Richard who is in a glowering mood. When he instructs her to sit, she does so without a word.

"On this very day," Richard begins, "that feline Flying Wallenda climbed to the top of Mrs. Matsui's five-hundred-year-old pine. The tippy top. Then he lost heart and began to cry. Piercing wails shattered the peace of the neighborhood. Everyone knows Ossie lives here, so please imagine my shame. I borrowed Mrs. Yomiyuri's twenty-foot, rotting, wood step ladder. I leaned the damn thing against the tree. Then I climbed the equivalent of two stories to a thin limb where your cat was stranded. I thought he was going to bite. Little did I know! But at this point he didn't even scratch. I placed Ossie under my arm until I reached an especially tacky moment in our descent. Then I put him on my shoulder. You needn't worry whether this was precarious for the cat because he simply dug in. Look!"

Richard opens his shirt and pulls it over his right shoulder, now perforated with small red holes.

"Needle and thread couldn't have fastened us better. In spite of this agony, I continued down. When we finally landed, the animal didn't let go. I bent to my knees and invited him to jump off. He did not. I descended on all fours, in full view of Mrs. Yomiyuri who was trying to hide behind her curtain. Meanwhile, Ossie walked slowly down my back. When he reached the base of my spine, he finally stepped off. Once on solid ground, his fear and trembling miraculously disappeared. He strutted and swaggered and paraded across the garden. Then Ossie turned his arrogant backside toward the porch and flooded the end of Mrs. Yomiyuri's magnificent home with the Great Salt Sea. Jane, Os is going. I'm sorry. In fact, I told Mrs. Yomiyuri he'd be gone by the end of the week."

Jane lets out a cry and heads for the door.

"Where are you going?" Richard demands.

"Lucy's."

For the first time she is prepared to call in a loan. She has escorted Lucy, advised her, translated for her, and endured a night at the club. Now it is time Lucy had a pet.

Jane passes the foul-smelling *benjo,* down the outside corridor with its cheap rooms hunkered side by side, and knocks at Lucy's door.

Lucy opens it, a towel wrapped around her head.

"Jane! What is it? Come in."

"Ossie needs a home," Jane says, still standing in the door. "It's desperate. Would you take him? All you have to do is let him sleep inside during the day and turn him loose at night. I'll help out. Buy food. I can't take him to the pound. Do you know what they call it here? The Japan Animal Welfare Society: JAWS." Jane begins to cry.

"Come in this minute," Lucy says. "Of course, I'll take him."

This isn't what Jane expected, and she thanks Lucy profusely through wet, stuttering sobs. Meanwhile, Lucy is patting her hand, offering kleenex and tea. She's concealed her talents as a nurse, or perhaps it's just the lack of opportunity, since no one would expect it of her or even ask.

The next day Jane brings Ossie over in a basket loaded with canned tuna and a catnip mouse he doesn't like. Lucy, with her preference for rainbows, examines the large orange tom and announces, "He's simply perfect." Apparently, she never noticed him when she came to visit.

"You know, Yoshi will just love him as a photographic subject."

★

Jane sees less of Lucy as her photographic activities become serious. Whenever she does, Lucy is full of news about Os whose pranks have turned harmless since he moved. Nowadays Lucy travels often with Yoshi on short photographic trips. They visit Nikko, Kamakura, the kilns at Hagi. They devote a full week to the Noto Peninsula. Whenever they are gone, Jane comes to feed the cat. Jane doesn't feel she knows Yoshi, except by word of mouth. She has only seen him twice since the coffee shop, both times accompanied by Lucy. Yet from the photographs in Lucy's room, Jane grows better acquainted.

They are in Hiroshima this week, and Jane is standing like a pilgrim before five new photos on Lucy's wall: a mendicant monk in straw sandals accepts coins from a video arcade; Pepsi Cola refreshes a family of four during their visit to the Heian shrine; two bent and toothless grandmothers gossip outside a glassy supermarket; a smiling fishmonger holds her catch up toward the camera's eye. And Ossie, dear old Os, arches up after napping in the stone lap of a god.

Jane suddenly cannot bear to stay in this room a moment longer.

★

Richard finds Jane lying on the tiny sofa, eyes wide open, her feet hanging over the end. He places his briefcase on the kitchen table. He's been in Tokyo all week.

"Is this a vision I see before me? Jane in a resting mode?"

She doesn't move or acknowledge that she's heard. He potters in the kitchen, removing iced tea from the fridge. Glass in hand, he joins her in the living room, sitting in the chair opposite the couch. He sits without moving. The air is still. The only sound is the tinkling of ice cubes in Richard's glass.

"Richard?" Jane says finally. "Have you ever noticed how some people are hounded by luck?"

"Are we talking about good luck or bad?"

Jane comes slowly to a sitting position, and Richard waits.

"You've been over to feed the cat, haven't you?" he says.

Jane nods.

"I never thought it was quite so simple," he says. " 'All nature is but art unknown to thee./All chance, direction which thou canst not see.' "

The room grows silent once again, until Jane releases a single tremulous sigh, a sound so deep one would think she'd been holding it all her life.

"Yes," she says quietly. "That would be me, wouldn't it? The one who cannot see."

In uncharacteristic slow-motion, she comes to her feet and leaves the room. Upstairs, her door slides shut with a small thud. She stands absolutely still in the midst of her clutter, trying in vain to conjure up the quiet room at Kimiko's.

Jane begins to tidy her desk, the books scattered on the windowsill, the school papers on the floor, driving back the looming hulk inside. She is so intent on her cleaning that she doesn't hear the tap on the door or the note being inserted somewhat later. She doesn't even see it until she is within hand's reach. She takes it out and reads: "Please open. Life hangs in the balance."

Jane opens the door with such force that the panels tremble. Richard is standing in the hall, his long torso leaning toward her like a butler's, hands clasped behind his back.

"I had in mind some *sushi,*" he says. "Rolls of handmade *norimaki*. Beautiful mounds of tuna, yellowtail, salmon. Whatever your heart desires."

For a moment she is afraid that she might cry, but Richard pretends not to see. He offers her the crook of his arm. She can feel the warmth and firmness of his grip as he steers her gently toward the stairs.

KITES

His daughter-in-law was spending too much time with the doctor. Fifteen minutes of consultation, and Tomura still sat in the examining room alone. The doctor had invited him to wait in the outer office while he talked with Amy, but Tomura said he'd stay where he was, if the doctor didn't mind. He was tired. Because of his checkup, he'd missed his nap.

A nurse came in to help him dress, a task Amy usually performed. His bent back made dressing painful, and to relieve the pain nowadays he walked around the block, every morning and evening. Once or twice he would stop and stretch himself up until, like a windblown reed, he leaned over again and continued along the street.

The nurse pulled the undershirt over his head. She was such a startling woman. So tall, with red cheeks and yellow hair. The sight of her vast bosom leaning toward him made him want to giggle like a schoolboy.

"I have reached the age of peace," he said, not caring that she couldn't understand a word. "Not even the doctor consults me anymore. He consults my relatives instead. Isn't that peaceful?"

The nurse nodded mechanically and announced in a voice like a train conductor, "Upsy-daisy, Mr. Tamara, honey."

Laughing, he took the kimono away from her and put it on, demonstrating with wordless flourish the proper wrap of the sash. He favored the kimono these days, thankful that none of the children said he looked funny. He used to wear Western clothes, even before coming to America, but now he found them binding. Tomura thought you could tell how frail a man was by the clothing he wore.

The nurse offered to help him out to the large front waiting room, but he shook his head. She left finally, and he was glad. Worn out, that's what he was. His skin felt dry and loose, as if, at any moment, it might shed. Even the grandchildren noticed. Noriko-chan, the youngest and sweetest and most American, was the first to tell him. So he began to notice, too, how his cheeks did not turn red even on the chilliest winter days.

Now the doctor went on and on with Amy, leaving him to guess the result. Liver? Stomach? Heart? He knew what the matter was. It had simply caught up with him, like a shadow bumping him rudely from behind. He stooped more as he walked, paused longer between tasks or between one position and another. He was even losing his appetite for Amy's food. Then sweet Noriko had asked, "Grandpa, how come you're so old?" He had laughed and tickled her, to make them both feel better.

★

Six years ago Tomura retired from his small Osaka business, visited the grave of his wife, and moved to California at his eldest son's request. Makoto told his father that he intended to stay. His wife Amy was already a citizen, since she'd been born here. Amy had gone out of her way to make Tomura feel at home. She spoke a shy Japanese, but she understood it well enough and was now taking lessons, at Makoto's urging. She introduced Tomura around a small circle of Japanese-Americans, a few of them parents as homesick as he.

He became particularly fond of a man named Ozawa. At one time the two old men spent hours together, arguing in the garden: whose chrysanthemums were rounder, sturdier, and held up better under the changeable Bay Area winds. Round and red-faced, Ozawa concealed his baldness under a Giants cap. It was Ozawa who regularly walked the three blocks, knocked, opened the door, and called out to any and all in the loud, cheerful voice of the mildly deaf, "Konnichi-wa, Tomura-sama!" Four years in a row, Ozawa had talked him into betting on the World Series, and for four years Tomura had lost.

When Ozawa died, Tomura didn't know how he could survive the loneliness again, were it not for Amy. She prodded Ozawa's widow Masae to continue the friendship, inviting her to join the family on outings here and there.

From time to time, Masae asked him to accompany her to a small shrine, a well-kept secret tucked into a residential area. The shrine was the occasional site of several ancient festivals, and young mothers of every color pushed their babies there. On spring evenings Tomura had noticed lovers embracing on stone benches beneath plum and cherry trees.

Amy once asked what it was he prayed for when he went there with Masae. He'd almost told her, too, but thought better of it. She would only take it as a rebuke, when none was intended. Instead, he told her he didn't ask for much, just continued good fortune with his family. Amy was embarrassed by his answer but pleased, he could tell. She never asked again.

Earlier in the week Amy had walked him to the streetcar stop where they met Masae Ozawa. How rosy her face was! Seeing her smile made him think of his own wife, dead so much longer than Ozawa. Masae's health was remarkable. What excellent posture too. When he asked what she did to maintain herself—what foods or potions or exercise—she laughed and reminded him that she was ten years younger. Surely that was the only reason.

Amy left them and they boarded the streetcar. Masae steadied him, guiding him into a seat. Then the car began its reassuring rock, and moved forward.

"Look at you, Kazuyuki-san," Masae teased. "Thin as a noodle, and such a good cook at your house too. Not like my house . . . I'll fatten you up. You need an old country diet. You should have a bit of radish every day, you know . . . Why don't we move in together? What do you think the children would say, huh? Think they're so modern!"

She had to stop, rub his back, because he'd begun to choke as he laughed.

Masae also lived with a son. It was her silence that told Tomura that things were not going well at her house. Masae had expressed her

hurt only once, when she'd allowed herself to call her son's wife
"stingy." In a voice reserved for concealed truths, she'd said that fathers-
in-law had an easier time of it.

"This world was not made for the comfort of women," she said
with exaggerated dignity.

He found it a puzzling remark. He would have to ask her about it
someday. Did anyone have a comfortable time of it? True, women had
cushioned his life. Yet how could anyone capable of so much care ever
feel its loss? So. He understood less than he thought. With her good
health she had everything to live for, and he asked her why she came to
the shrine.

"I pray for peace at home," she answered. "I used to be very
angry, and you see? Things have gotten better. I have lovely grandchildren. What would we do without the grandchildren, huh?" She
laughed and poked him in the side.

What a remarkable confession. Masae angry? He couldn't imagine it.

They stopped at a restaurant before continuing on foot to the
shrine. Masae knew the owner, and he seated them at a comfortable private booth. She ordered for them both, fussing over him as she poured
his tea, arranged his bowl. Why didn't they do more things together?

At the shrine, they stood apart. He didn't want to overhear Masae's
prayers, or to be overheard. When he closed his eyes, he saw Amy's
face. She had enough to do without him . . .

Tomura tried to be helpful. He pulled weeds, snapped green beans,
watched the grandchildren. He'd recently polished Amy's silver, marveling at the heavy, expensive utensils that tarnished not only themselves
but the taste of his food. But none of this was enough. When Noriko
was old enough for school, Amy would have some time. Still he worried. Makoto was seldom home. The flush of interest between the
couple seemed to have vanished with Noriko's arrival. Rather abruptly,
he remembered. Now, out of necessity, his son buried himself in work
and Amy with the children. Was he mistaken, or was Makoto becoming gruff?

Tomura clapped twice. Masae was standing just in front of the bell
rope, Tomura to one side. When she'd finished, she pulled the rope,
and the praying was over. In a small kiosk, they purchased folded paper

fortunes. They read them and then tied them to nearby trees. White
bows covered the small plums growing in the shrine courtyard, and
from a distance the trees looked like sculptures of papier-maché. Worn
out, they rested on a stone bench, bowing first to an elderly couple
already seated at one end. Masae began chatting with the other woman.
Masae is a woman of many accomplishments, he told himself, listening
to her unhesitant English. As the women talked, Tomura noticed how
the other old man nodded in the sun like an ancient lizard.

Masae helped Tomura up from the bench. They decided it might
be wise to take a taxi. During the trip home, he dozed in the back, his
chin resting against his chest while his cane formed a third leg. When
they reached the house, Masae waited with him in the front room to
greet Amy. Amy had heard them come in and joined them. She invited
the older woman to stay for tea, but Masae declined. Amy insisted she
come later in the week, and Masae accepted. Tomura was thrilled. He
hoped the invitation was sincere. He hoped it wouldn't be too much of
a chore for Amy. He would offer to help, and this time they wouldn't
tell his son.

Several months before, when Masae had come to visit, Makoto
was scandalized for some unknown reason. Instead of saying anything
to his father, Makoto scolded his wife for an impropriety she couldn't
understand. After all, his mother had been gone for years, and Tomura
himself was fragile.

"He's hardly having an affair," Amy had said. "And if he is, what
business is it of ours?" The old man heard them from his room, heard
the slap, the cry, and Makoto stomping up to the second floor. When
there was silence, he made his tentative way to Amy. He saw the red
mark at the corner of her mouth and gasped.

"What has he done to you?" he said, his voice thin with anger.

"Not to worry," Amy said consolingly. "It's nothing, really. He
won't do it again."

Tomura hadn't been consoled. Over and over, he thought to himself, I don't recognize this son. Had he ever slapped his wife? The
thought that he might have upset him so much that he stopped where
he was and sat down. Perhaps Ozawa was the lucky one.

★

"Father?" Amy stood in the doorway of the examining room. Tomura rose to his feet with the help of his cane.

"So," he said, lightheartedly. "Is the long consultation over?" The doctor met them at the door. Tomura thought the doctor looked rather ill himself. Bloated.

"Nothing important or new," the doctor said. "You're much the same. Keep exercising. Avoid too much salt or tobacco."

"I don't smoke," the old man said.

He bowed and thanked the doctor. As they left, Amy took his arm.

"Together we make one and a half people," he joked, but Amy wasn't amused.

The air outside was cool for April, but the late afternoon sun felt good against his eyes. Warm light reflected off tile roofs and stucco walls while soft blue shadows formed between the bungalows. As they passed the schoolyard, he saw boys at the far end flying kites. A light, gusty wind picked up the brightly colored discs, dragons, airplanes, and fierce samurai heads. From a distance, he heard a kite tail snap, heard the small boys' voices yelling through the uneven breeze.

Suddenly, one kite lost the current and plunged head first into the grass a few yards from where Tomura stood. A colt-legged boy dashed to the kite and yelled something to his friends that Tomura couldn't understand. The kite was unharmed. The boy wound up the string, running back across the field. The kite head bounced behind him like a flat balloon until a breeze lifted it up. It pulled away, bobbing and dancing, and the boy yelled in triumph.

Tomura cheered, waving his cane in the air. Amy whirled around and gasped. She moved toward him, afraid he might topple over, then stopped. He was laughing, his face lit by fire.

"Father?" she said at last. "Don't you think we should go home? It's getting cold."

. . . Where had it come from, this moment of unexpected joy? Amy was saying something, but he didn't need to hear. He stared out across the schoolyard, remembering the boy he'd once loved to watch, racing through their narrow cobbled street. He stretched his body up and held himself straight, his back reaching for the kites as though pulled by a string.

SAKURAJIMA

1

Marta hadn't imagined what a mistake it might be, taking the night boat from Okinawa to Japan. A short sea trip had seemed like such a good idea, an adventure, a short and much-needed rest. Especially after the long year of teaching in Taiwan. She'd been so surrounded by well-wishers in the Taipei airport, so overwhelmed with gifts, students pressing their addresses into her hand, that she must have been in a state of euphoria when she left.

Only after she'd boarded the ship in Naha did she realize the tourist berth was a single, open room. A hundred travelers shared space on a raised *tatami* surface, heads laid to rest against pillows of stone. Throughout the night, adults snored, children whimpered, and the lights never dimmed. Sleep was impossible, and Marta Lash fled to an empty deck where nothing but flying fish disturbed a soothing and monotonous sea.

The ship docked in Kagoshima after breakfast, but she'd felt much too done in to eat. Kimura, who met her, must have sensed how tired she was. He took her at once to the oceanfront hotel and said he'd be back for her at two. He hadn't changed. She couldn't remember exactly how long ago it was since she'd last seen him in the States, leading his group of students. Five years, maybe. She preferred not to remember herself as she was then or how she had behaved. She had been forced to share her upstairs bathroom with two of Kimura's boys, and her company-loving mother had had to remind her daily not to be rude.

Marta showered and rested before opening the hotel drapes. From the bed she could see white plumes lift up from the mouth of a shapely volcano, and drift westward, a strip of sea separating the volcano from the mainland. Small boats pulled through this narrow channel as a high morning sun concentrated the colors of sea and sky into rich, exuberant blues. *Lava makes the island soil rich. Farmers raise daikon radishes the length of stalactites, cabbages the size of pumpkins.* Who it was that had told her this? Kimura probably. Tomorrow he would take her over, if the weather remained fair. But who could tell? It was the rainy season— *tsuyu,* Kimura called it—and the atmosphere was unstable. To Marta, the bright, calm sky looked incapable of bad weather.

In the quiet of the hotel room, she felt herself letting go, the plea- sure of solitude, lost for months, finally restored.

★

How curious it had seemed to her even then—a self-absorbed schoolgirl—the way her mother had specialized in defeated nations. One year, the family had hosted a young Irish track star. The next year, two German girls. Finally, when she was a college junior, Kimura's boys had visited, and her brother Joe, who ought to have been there, was out of town. (Joe had missed the Germans too, although Mother was probably glad that he had. When Marta's parents were out, one of the German girls had smuggled a boyfriend into her room. To Marta's astonishment, her soft-spoken mother confronted Renata the next day in a righteous fury. Instead of taking her lumps, Renata screamed and wept and accused her compatriot of tattling. When the woman from the Michigan American Friends Service phoned the following summer, her mother requested boys. Ordered them, Marta had thought, like a catered meal.)

She couldn't remember two more awkward young men. The Jap- anese group had arrived in a flurry of bows and miscued entrances, and the boys couldn't decide who should enter the house first, as if the first one to enter was surely going to his death. Even the luggage was a problem. Both boys staggered under the weight of large, blocky suitcases, grunting and scraping up the stairs and down the long hardwood hall. (If it had been Joe or she, the trail of disfiguring scuff marks would *not* have gone unremarked.) The language that flashed out of their mouths had a pleasant staccato sound. Marta liked the round Japanese vowels and compact syllables. She hadn't much cared for the sound of German, all damp and growling, like Renata.

At six on the first evening of their stay, the boys were summoned to dinner but didn't appear. Unaccustomed to waiting, her father looked at his watch. The boys were called again, and Marta was sent to find them. They were in their room. Yes, they smiled, they'd heard the call, but they were finishing a game of chess and would come down later.

"I don't think you understand," Marta said. "They want you down now. You can come back later and finish."

The lean boy, Kinnosuke, stared at her. "Why?" he asked. Noboru, the sturdy one, said they'd be right there. He spoke rapidly to Kino, as they'd decided to call him, and then followed Marta downstairs. Several minutes later Kino appeared, puzzled and sullen. Marta's father glared at him with unconcealed annoyance.

"Shall we start again, boys?" he said. "Here you come to the table as soon as you're called." Marta had never heard him sound so unpleasant.

They stared into their plates as Mrs. Lash passed green beans and fried chicken, her voice too loud and gay. Throughout the meal, they kept their heads bent close to their food, like a pair of penitent orphans, and Kino made such a revolting sucking noise that Marta couldn't bear to finish. When the meal was finally over and her mother had excused them, they stood up together, bowed to her father, and fled.

"Has Dad gone off his rocker?" she asked her mother later.

"Just give him time."

"He wasn't that way with the Germans."

"That was different. They were girls."

"Well, he wasn't that way with Desmond either."

"You just don't remember, dear. All that blarney! Desmond flattered your father."

The week that followed crawled slowly out of the cellar of that first meal. Home for the summer, Marta was off each morning to a job at the library, leaving her mother to entertain the boys, if necessary. No one seriously expected her father to become involved at all. Ordinarily, the boys' days were organized, and a van would come to pick them up. Noboru was the first out the door. Minutes later, Kino would appear, having left the scene of some mishap. His watch was missing. He'd misplaced his glasses after his shower. Had anyone seen his dictionary?

Since there was absolutely nothing they could do to make Kino prompt for meals, they usually started without him. ("Beat him! Flail him! Cut off his head!" Marta chanted whenever her father got huffy.)

The boys were out when her mother remarked, "I'm afraid our Kino is floundering."

It was true, but what could they do? Trying to converse with Kino was like talking to yourself. Noboru, who was as unobtrusive as a household pet, joined the family as if he were immersing himself in a refreshing pool. Always attentive, he listened and watched and spoke when spoken to, as if his eyes and ears and head were synchronized into some marvelous, and marveling, recorder. It wasn't at all like that for Kinnosuke. He would appear at the edge of the family and ask the most tiresome questions: the spelling of states, the pronunciation of verbs that no one ever used, the meaning of some outdated idiom that he had just discovered in his school text. What would happen if someone hid his silly schoolbook? Would he wither away like some cursed child in a fairy tale? You'd think his books were the only things he trusted.

"Don't you ever stop studying?" Marta teased as he sat hunched in one corner of a sofa.

Kino pulled back his thin bird shoulders and looked past her to the wall.

"We Japanese have to study hard. We have so many exams to pass before we can go to university."

Marta felt annoyed, lectured. If this was so, why wasn't Noboru's head stuck in a book too?

"Do you know what Kino said to me?" she announced later to her mother, muddling her *l*'s and *r*'s, quoting him in a far heavier accent than he had ever used. "I think he's a crashing bore," Marta finished.

"Perhaps it's harder for him," Mrs. Lash replied. "I had a phone call from Mr. Kimura. He was checking up. I told him things were fine, and I suppose they are, after a fashion. I didn't mention that first

day. I did say I thought things were difficult for Kino. He understood.
Then he said they were very proud of Kinnosuke. Isn't that odd? Seems
they put him with Noboru deliberately."

"Why?" Marta asked.

"I don't know, dear. I didn't ask, and he didn't volunteer."

★

The Bijou was packed. Only by some aggressive maneuvering did
Marta get the boys in at all. She'd been delighted when she saw the theater ads, bragging that *The Gold Rush* hadn't been shown in a decade.
Chaplin would be perfect for the boys. She'd even taken it upon herself
to rush them through dinner so they'd reach the theater on time, and
now they could hardly see the screen. It made her absolutely fierce, the
way some film buffs could be so rude—towering up, blocking people's
view with their huge, unpruned shrubs of hair! She didn't know why
she remained so upset since it didn't matter to Kino anyway. He'd
dropped off as soon as the house lights went down. It was after nine
when they got home, and Kino went straight to bed.

"Kino missed it all," she told her mother scornfully. "From start to
finish."

"He's not used to staying up late," Noboru said quickly. "He grew
up on a farm. His mother gets up at three, maybe four every morning.
So Kinnosuke-san gets up too, and studies."

It was a soft rebuke, mild enough to make Marta feel sorry that
Kino had missed the fun. Maybe he was used to missing things, growing up on a farm. (Why hadn't she known this before?) Maybe there
were chores he was expected to do, until she remembered something
Noboru had said: "Studying is our chore." How would it feel to be
transported to Kino's farm and have to get up at four? No, it was beyond imagining.

"I have something to show you," Noboru said, and returned
shortly with photographs and postcards. Here was Kagoshima, he nar-
rated. Here, the tip of Kyushu. Marta looked through the pictures one
by one, through farmland and resorts, castles, cypress, seascapes. Yes,
she said politely, it must be a lovely place to live, but somehow the pictures conveyed no special reality, told surprisingly little of his life. They

were like cheerfully bright magazine prints of tundra, exotic tropical birds and antelope, which one admired without ever sensing the place.

"Here's Sakurajima. It's on an island across from the city." He handed her a postcard of a volcano, embedded in the sea.

"Is it active?" she asked. He looked puzzled. "Alive," she said.

"Yes." He laughed. "It's alive. When you come to visit, we'll take you there."

He handed her another postcard: an islander in a bright kimono and white headband held up a huge vegetable she couldn't identify. "The farmers on the island grow the longest radishes," he said proudly. "And the fattest cabbages—like pumpkins. It's the lava. You'll see."

★

The boys' stay had stretched into its third and final week when the heat fell like a stiff wool blanket across the city. Cooling systems, seldom called upon, pumped and gasped and occasionally broke down. Tempers flared in public, even in the library. The reading rooms had remained comfortable, but the narrow stacks and small offices grew stuffy and hot. Marta returned from work on such a day—the boys were at the Natural History Museum, her mother said—and went immediately to her room. It was much too warm to close the door.

Marta took a record and placed it on her stereo. Wretched and damp, she flopped into an old leather recliner. She listened, as always, with the base of the recliner thrust out, her feet up, eyes closed, until she found again what she thought of as her 'secret ledge behind the falls.' Here she was cool and dry and soothed by the rushing melodies that fell freely and powerfully, as if from the top of a gorge. She became aware of someone else in the room, a dimming of light, an unconscious breathing, as if the sound of falling water had changed pitch.

She opened her eyes and saw Kinnosuke in the doorway, staring vaguely toward the stereo, a book clasped against his chest. The sharp, primitive urge to chase him out left when she noticed he was paying rapt attention to the music, not her.

"Come in," she said, righting the recliner and pointing to her desk chair. "Sit down."

Kino murmured a thank-you and sat cross-legged on the floor. The record was nearing its end; one final band began. They listened as the pianist

took the arpeggios and runs with the precision of a sentient clock. She let the
needle lift and come to rest, then handed him the record sleeve.

"Do you like Chopin?" she asked.

"Yes," he said, reading, the sleeve drawn up close to his nose.

"Do you play?"

"No, but my younger sister plays." He continued reading.

"Then you must have a piano at home."

"Yes. My mother found one for her. An older one, but it's very
nice for my sister."

"I studied for years," she said.

"Oh? Do you still play?" He glanced at her.

"No. I wasn't very good, as it turned out. To tell you the truth, I'd
rather listen."

Marta turned the record over, and they listened in silence.
Chopin's magic somehow righted the confusion of her day — the misplaced books, the patrons irritated with their fines, the gray and tattered
transients, the regulars who came each day for the coolness or the newspapers or the chairs. Even the intolerable heat seemed unimportant, and
she wondered if Kino felt the same.

"Marta!" her mother called from the bottom of the stairs.

"Gotta go," she said. "You can stay and play some more if you like."

For the first time, he looked at her directly, his eyes blinking.

"That's very kind, but I better not. I have some reading to do." He
got to his feet hurriedly and slipped out of the room.

★

"I'll say this for the Japanese," her father said. "They certainly
know how to spoil their children."

The heat had not abated, and Mr. Lash started the car, the air running, even though neither boy was in sight. Suddenly, Noboru burst
out of the house.

"Sorry," he said, climbing in back beside Marta.

"And where is Kino-san?" Lash trumpeted.

"He's coming. He's looking for his tie."

Five minutes of tepid circulating air passed before Kino appeared.
Lash was speechless with rage. It was only a short ride, Mrs. Lash
reminded him, and the dinner hour was flexible. But the fact of the

matter was, he complained, they were going to be late. They would be
the last to arrive. They would keep the others waiting. A businessman
of Brice Smith's stature was undoubtedly used to the strictest punctual-
ity! The car grew still as his voice rose. Marta hoped that at least his re-
marks were beyond the reach of the boys.

All together, fourteen families were involved, but Marta counted
only six cars, including their own. Aura Smith met them at the door.

"Why, Harold. You do run a tight ship. I've been getting calls all
day from host families. They're all having trouble getting their students
organized." She laughed, as if it were all a wonderful joke.

Families dribbled in, and the students nestled into a group, happy
to see one another, comfortable at last. One family was late by nearly an
hour, and Marta nudged her father when they arrived. A petite girl
looked near to tears when she walked through the door. Her compatriots squealed, and the mood pulling down her face vanished.

The adults moved off in the direction of a long, white living room,
sipping wine. Soon Aura Smith invited the young people to the buffet
table. Marta heard a voice behind her say, "Watch out. They'll pick it
clean," and was too embarrassed to turn around. The students chose
sparingly. So sparingly that Aura Smith, who had stationed herself at the
end of the buffet, stopped several on their way out.

"My dear, that isn't enough to feed a bird. You'll come back? Get
more?"

Host brothers and sisters joined the students on a patio strung with
paper lanterns, but Marta stayed indoors, safe from the heat and demands of the poking, playful students. She hadn't wanted to come at
all, saw no need for her appearance, but her mother had looked so
upset when she told her that Marta simply caved in. Several Japanese
adults mingled with the families. They had accompanied the students
from Kyushu, she heard Aura say.

"Not just chaperones. More like surrogate parents."

Yes, it did seem that way, and perhaps that is what these students
needed, especially Kino. All he seemed to need was to be told what to
do, where to go, what to wear. Kino was always just behind you or off
to one side—waiting, waiting. But for what? Mother might have been
able to tell him what to do, but how could she? She never coddled Joe,

and she certainly wasn't about to start in now on these boys, even if she had known how.

The summer light faded, and the students came indoors. Brice Smith set up a slide projector and screen. Host fathers drew up chairs while students arranged themselves on the floor in front. Noboru came forward and joined a tall, long-faced boy named Takashi. From the back of Takashi's head, a cowlick fanned out of control.

Before leaving home, Takashi explained, students had prepared slides of their families. The girls, all blushes and giggles, the boys, solemn-faced, each came to the front and explained the scene on the screen, their background, their plans for the future.

Kino rose and spoke in his soft, careful English. The slide showed a woman in a black ceremonial kimono. She knelt beside the hearth of an old farmhouse, preparing tea. She looked old enough to be Kino's grandmother. Kino explained that his father was not at home when the slides were taken. He worked at a factory a hundred miles away, to supplement income at the farm. Kino had eight brothers and sisters, and he was the next to youngest. One sister remained at home with the mother. Another slide appeared, a serious Kino with his elderly mother and young, plain sister—the piano player.

"I'll take my exams next year," he said. "If I pass, I'll be the first in my family to attend a university. I want to teach English one day."

One picture blended into another, one student into the next, and Marta lost track. Somber parents and somber child. An uncluttered living room here, a tidy, blooming garden there. Over and over in her mind she saw the old mother beside the hearth, pouring tea for the last of her sons—the one who wished to be a teacher.

Noboru stood. In his confident English he told the group that he was the son of a businessman, a *sake* merchant, that he had one younger brother at home, and that he hoped to study international law.

A portrait of two elegantly robed parents appeared on the screen. The setting was light: sand-colored *tatami,* white walls, a single lily in a vase that stood alone, in an alcove. Noboru's mother was as elaborately coiffed as a *geisha* and both parents were playing long, lacquered *kotos,* in a scene of reassuring and calculated refinement.

The lights came up, and the room exploded with talk. Takashi announced that the students would like to perform a few traditional songs.

Kinnosuke Katawara would lead the group. Marta sat forward abruptly in her folding chair. Kino? Her mother was leaning forward too.

"Katawara-san has perfect pitch," Takashi said. "We can't sing a thing without him."

Why hadn't Kino sung at home, or did he wait until everyone had gone? She felt something quick and sharp, a small pain of exclusion from news others shared.

Kino sang one clear, sustained note. The students began "Sakura," the cherry blossom song, singing slowly in a minor key as though performing a dirge. It amazed her that something named for a flower could be so melancholy. Kino announced another song. Like the tune itself, the voices were light and airy and unmemorable. There was a buzz of talk, a decision being made, some kind of hand-waving and denial. Takashi announced that Katawara-san would sing a solo. It had been Kino waving his hands in that unmistakable no, until Noboru whispered in his ear. Kino turned to the others, instructing them in something, and turned back to the audience.

"This is a very old folk song called 'Aka Tomba,' 'Red Dragonfly.' "

He closed his eyes as if searching for the note. As soon as he began to sing, his discomfort vanished, and a sound as beautifully haunting as a wood flute filled the room. He held the long notes until their end, the tones never wavering, the voice as pure as a choirboy's. Tears of admiration and surprise stung Marta's eyes, and she clapped long and hard, long after the others had stopped. But Kino had disappeared to the back. Noboru and Takashi pulled him to the front for his bow alone.

The students returned to the patio in a giggling lump as adults stood and stretched and drifted toward the dining room for coffee. Marta was unable to move.

Cups tinked politely in saucers as Smith rose to introduce Kimura-san. Mr. Lash leaned over to his wife and whispered, "This will be the Chamber of Commerce portion of the evening."

"Honorable friends," Kimura began.

Marta heard the record player in the distance, a few girlish squeals. The young people were visible through an expanse of plate glass, their figures etched by lantern light.

". . . and all are serious students," Kimura was saying. "The best in their schools, chosen by their teachers to come to America. In one of your homes, we have a young girl whose father wept at the airport and said to me, 'Look after her, please. She's my youngest.' In another of your homes, we have our wealthiest and poorest students, together. These are our future, our flowers, who have grown up in the soil of Sakurajima . . ."

Outside, the students had taken up a game of claps and chants, and Marta strained to hear them. Kimura and the entire room of adults dimmed swiftly as if moved to a remote corner of the house. *"Ichi, ni, san, shi,"* the young people repeated again and again, the words a string of pearls passed among them. *"Ichi, ni, san, shi . . ."* Perhaps, in a moment, if she were patient, they would sing again, and she might hear once more that nightingale voice rising up from the dark, clear and unafraid.

2

After graduation, Marta had accepted a job in Taiwan, teaching English at a woman's college. Marta's own college friend Mary Chang had encouraged her to go, helping her with the arrangements. Mary had suggested that, en route, Marta take some time in Tokyo. Once she reached Taiwan, Marta would find little time to rest. She would begin teaching immediately, and it was very hot.

"Rest up," Mary advised. "See the sights. Tokyo is very cosmopolitan. Taichung is not."

Reluctantly, Marta scheduled a layover. She felt prepared for the nine months of teaching, mostly because people like Mary, more capable than herself, had made the arrangements. It was her first foreign trip, and the thought of tackling Japan as well as Taiwan had made her feel uneasy.

In preparation for the brief layover in Japan, Marta wrote both Kinnosuke Katawara and Noboru Sakai. Noboru didn't answer, but her letter to Kino had been forwarded from his mother's farm in Kagoshima Prefecture to Tokyo, where Kino was attending a small university she'd never heard of.

He was studying French now, he wrote, as well as English. He planned to teach both someday. He was very busy with his studies and his two *arbeiten,* but he would be happy to meet his American sister. He included his rooming house phone number. "And how is my American mother?" he wrote. Kino never inquired about her father in any of his letters, and her own memories of Kino had become so misshapen that she could only muster the feeblest pleasure at having someone in Tokyo to phone.

Once she had arrived, a stylish young woman at the Tokyo Tourist Bureau told her to stop anyone who looked like a student. "They'll be glad to help," she reassured Marta, in passable English. And so they were, almost to excess. One schoolgirl stopped to chat while Marta was peering through an antique store window, somewhere off the Ginza. The girl concluded her conversation by asking, "Do you prefer apples or oranges?" The experience reminded her of Kinnosuke.

The day before her flight to Taipei, she finally called him. Kino would come to the hotel.

Marta went downstairs at 7:00 p.m. The lobby was a remarkably small area for a hotel so large, as if the management wished to discourage loitering. She waited on a short, plump sofa that provided a clear view of the entrance. At 7:15 a young man confronted the revolving doors and began to push the wrong way. He gave the door such a jolt his glasses fell to the pavement. A group of departing guests blocked her view, and she turned her attention to the desk, where a delegation of Indians all spoke at once in fast, imperious voices. When she looked back, Kinnosuke was standing beside her.

"You've grown," she said, meaning to sound sisterly.

"Yes," he said. "I recognized you right away, Marta. You look the same." It had been four years since she'd seen him, when he had been such a reluctant guest in her home.

He was several inches taller, but still thin. The face was more mature, the cheekbones sharper, the hair better groomed. Even his glasses seemed more manly, but one of the lenses was cracked near the frame.

He'd traveled quite a distance, from the north end of Tokyo. After she'd phoned, she'd looked it up on a map.

"How is your mother?" he inquired, and Marta answered that she was well. "I think your mother is a very kind person," he said.

His own parents now lived with an older brother, who ran the farm.

"It seems we've both become teachers," she said when the subject of families had been exhausted. "Did I tell you I'd be teaching in Taiwan?"

"Yes," he said without looking at her. "It sounds interesting."

He didn't sound interested, as if he couldn't imagine what it would be like for her. He'd left Japan as a boy and traveled halfway around the world before she'd ever left the States. Now he sat still and polite and uncomprehending. Perhaps his mind was too much on his studies.

"What's an *arbeit?*" she asked. "You mentioned it in your letter."

"A part-time job. It's a German word, I believe."

"And you have two?"

"Yes. I look after the rooming house, and I tutor French. *Parlez-vous français?*"

"*Un peu.* It's been years."

"*Quelle belle langue, n'est-ce pas? Je préfère le français. Comprenez-vous?*"

"Do you mind if we use English? I'm very tired."

"*Je comprends.*"

"I'd like to take you out to eat."

"*Merci.*"

"But I must ask you to recommend a place."

"We can find something nearby," he said.

Relieved, she picked up her purse. Kinnosuke reclaimed the umbrella that had fallen between his knees to the floor. As he leaned forward, the arm clasping the umbrella moved as if attached to another body, and the handle struck him in the forehead. "It's all right," he said before she could ask. She led him toward the revolving entrance.

"I'll go first," she suggested. "You follow in the next space." And they reached the street without incident.

"You'll have to guide me, I'm afraid," she said.

"I seldom come here. It's too far."

"What do you recommend?"

"I really don't know."

Like the quick, hot jab of a needle, she felt that old anger she'd felt for Kino the highschool student, and then it was gone.

They walked past tightly packed shops: record stores; *pachinko* parlors; cinemas and bars and coffee shops; a tall, narrow building that rose in tiers, each floor a different luxury restaurant. Kino was speaking in his annoying mix of English and French when she noticed a display case for a second-story restaurant. It was snack-shop fare: ham and cheese sandwiches, spaghetti, curried rice, fruit, and ice cream dishes. All of it looked bland and clean, artfully displayed and duplicated in a dozen other windows she'd seen during her walks through the Ginza.

"This one?" she asked. It was clear now that he'd been waiting for her to choose.

They climbed the narrow, carpeted stairs and took a table near the back, beside a window that overlooked the street. A bored waiter with a tall, slick pompadour handed them menus that Kinnosuke seemed as incapable of understanding as she. Single English words were printed under the Japanese, and she found the word *spaghetti*. She'd heard the word several times in the last few days, with a pleasant Japanese lilt.

They gave their orders, and Marta asked where he planned to teach. Tokyo? Or would he return to Kyushu? He answered in French and translated into English. Marta drank hurriedly and long from a glass of iced coffee, drowning the urge to snap. It was her fault, really. She shouldn't have admitted to knowing a word of French. But how was she to know he'd pester her with it?

"Do you ever see Noboru Sakai?" she asked. She'd been reluctant to ask, hoping he would volunteer some news.

"Have you heard from his family?" Kino asked.

"No. That's just it. I wrote. My mother wrote, but we haven't heard a thing."

She tried to imagine Noboru now, older but still poised. He would know his way around, know how to order a meal, unflustered by the presence of a guest.

If nothing else, she must get Noboru's number and phone before she left.

"I'm sorry to be the one to tell you," Kino said. "I believe Sakai was in some sort of traffic accident. He was a student at Todai. You know Todai?" Marta nodded.

Had he graduated already? An alarming stillness filled the space between them.

"Yes? Was he hurt?"

"I'm afraid he was killed. I'm sorry."

Marta stared at Kinnosuke. His eyes were fixed on the oblong plate of spaghetti. From the restaurant stereo, a girlish voice sang a popular Japanese song. The waiter passed, and the scent of curry lingered behind.

"When?"

"It was the year we were freshmen. Three years ago."

Soft lights shadowed a young couple huddled at a corner table, their shoulders touching, ankles crossed. Someone laughed on their way down the stairs and out. Somewhere below, in the street, a van honked, a muted electronic beep. From the window, she could see a group of students stopping by a book stall, another paying for a movie.

Kinnosuke ate his spaghetti noisily. She remembered his noise, unsubdued from the day he had arrived to the day he left. Someone must have told Noboru that meal noise wasn't an American custom. Noboru was always quiet at meals, observant, and now, in this city of millions, quiet for all time.

"Do you still sing?" she asked. His cheeks reddened.

"Sometimes. With my friends. But I don't have much time."

"The other students thought very highly of your singing."

"It's not very good, really."

Incredible. His voice had been his one shining talent, and now he was too modest to speak of it, as though it were a cause of embarrassment and not delight.

"You knew more songs than the other students, didn't you? Noboru told me your mother taught you old songs no one else knew."

"Country songs, yes. None of the other students were from the country."

"But they admired those songs, Kino."

"Perhaps."

"And they asked you to sing that lovely song, alone. What was it? 'Aka Tomba?'"

"Yes, but every school child knows 'Aka Tomba.'"

He was running away from her.

"Did you ever think of teaching music?" she asked. For a moment, he brightened.

"Yes. Once. But I would have to teach in elementary school. I want to teach in a high school or college. If I teach English and French, there are more jobs. Better jobs. I have to think of my future."

Yes, the future. That was no longer Noboru's concern. If he'd lived, it would not have been his concern either. His future had been assured from the start. The family. The university. It was all secure, but not for Kino. She saw that now.

"I wonder if we could speak French for just a little while," Kino said behind a vanishing noodle. "I need lots of practice."

She didn't hear him. She had been watching the gentle eyes behind the glasses. She'd never noticed his eyes before, their depth.

3

Kimura returned to the hotel to pick her up at two, as promised. Inside the chauffeured car, Kimura-san spoke with Takashi Fukui, while Marta waited in the back seat. All grown up, she thought. This Takashi in no way resembled the tall, funny boy of five summers ago, the boy whose hair used to stand straight up. She remembered that he'd been something of a leader among the summer students, like Noburo.

Her year in Taiwan had passed so quickly that only in the last weeks, taking her mother's advice, had she written Takashi and Kimura-san. (She'd seen no point in writing Kino. This time her Tokyo layover would last only a few hours, just long enough to change planes.) It did seem the thing to do, however, to visit Kagoshima on her way back to the States. She thought it unlikely she'd have another chance.

Takashi was turning toward her, his English as flawless as Kimura's.

"We just wanted to warn you, Marta. Mr. Sakai sometimes cries when he talks about Noboru. We never know. Noboru was his first son."

"I understand," she said.

"Please don't let it upset you. They're very eager to meet you."

The car stopped across from the Sakai family home, a traditional dwelling with a blue-tiled roof and the obligatory wood wall separating it from the street. From where they were parked, no one could tell much about its occupants. The street was in the heart of the old city, the address effectively concealing the Sakai family's wealth.

Mrs. Sakai answered the door. She bowed to the floor, elaborately greeting the two men, then Marta. A plump woman, she wore a plain Western dress in a pattern of somewhat lumpy, pastel flowers. Marta remembered the slide of Noboru's elegant mother, dressed in a brocade kimono.

Mrs. Sakai led them through the house to a room that overlooked a small, well-tended garden. Gardenia bushes stood thick with blooms. Ferns plumed up beside a large black rock and around an oblong pool filled with orange and white carp. Mr. Sakai was out back, she explained through Takashi, called out on wine business. He would be in directly. Marta arranged herself on the floor cushion, her legs awkwardly folded to one side, while Mrs. Sakai sat with her feet tucked neatly beneath her.

Sakai appeared and the elaborate greeting was repeated. Mrs. Sakai brought in tea things: special rice and seaweed crackers, dried fish unique to the city, small moist bean cakes that stuck like clay in Marta's throat.

In the wall to her right stood a family shrine, crowded with memorabilia. Photos, toys, dried flowers, and burnt incense cluttered the cabinetlike altar, with its tablet of scripture and small brass Buddha. Everything appeared faded and fixed in time.

"Would you like to inquire about the altar?" Takashi asked. He'd been watching her, she realized, anticipating. His English had grown solemn.

"Yes, please."

A long exchange followed. Kimura tensed and straightened himself on his knees. Perhaps they shouldn't have asked. Perhaps this was the moment when the grief broke through. Takashi turned to Marta— Sakai sat silent, head bowed—telling her about the shrine to Sakai's son, the promising Tokyo University student who was a passenger in a car that hit a stone wall in the countryside outside Tokyo. (Takashi handed her a picture.) Here was the exact spot. The students in front were killed instantly. Those in back were injured but lived. They'd placed a wreath, later a small planter of flowers that still marked the spot on the wall. The family kept flowers in their shrine—(Takashi pointed)—and on a small statue near the home, a bust of Ojizu-san, the god of children.

"We'll pass the statue when we leave," Takashi added quietly. "It's not far. Around the corner."

Marta offered her sympathy. "I'm afraid I didn't know until last year, when I passed through Tokyo. Kinnosuke Katawara told me."

This news was received in silence, and for a moment she could think of nothing more to say. To her relief, Takashi picked up where she had left off, speaking quietly and earnestly with Mrs. Sakai. Did they remember Kinnosuke, she wondered? A thin, studious boy with horn-rim glasses, now a somewhat taller, studious young man with thicker glasses? Awkward Kinnosuke. Kino hadn't wanted to tell her. She'd had to bring Noboru up. At the time, she'd wondered if the ancient Japanese killed their bearers of bad news, like the Greeks.

Mrs. Sakai said her other son would join them. As she spoke, a striking young man in a blue summer kimono entered the room, bowed, and sat down. He was taller, more elegant-looking, and suddenly she couldn't remember what Noboru looked like at all.

"He's a student at Keio University," Takashi explained.

So the Sakai boys had done well. Both had gone up to Tokyo, like the promising sons of an old Southern family in the States, heading north to Harvard and Princeton.

The young man looked bored, sullen. For an uncomfortable moment, Marta wondered if he disliked her presence. Perhaps he simply disliked Americans, or perhaps all this talk of Noboru darkened his face. He made no effort to conceal his distaste at being in a room of mourners and rememberers, even though he hadn't said a word. (Why Noboru and not this boy?) Maybe this was only the way young Keio University men behaved, a studied and irritating indifference that everyone but herself understood and forgave. Maybe it was all a young man's self-preserving posture. She could only remember Noboru's brightness, his geniality, during those weeks, five years ago. This other son would still have been a child. Could it be that Noboru's behavior might only have been another kind of posture? The posture of a guest?

"Sakai-san is interested in anything you might remember about his son," Takashi was saying.

"Yes, of course." Kimura looked relieved, but where to begin? Hadn't Noboru told them everything? Surely a Japanese son would at least tell his mother the details of the house, family, kitchen, food. Perhaps repetition didn't matter, or mattered greatly, the repeated story celebrating a life briefly lived. Her memories were what they were after, but where to begin?

"I once took Noboru and Kinnosuke to see a Charlie Chaplin movie," she began. *"The Gold Rush,* it was called . . ."

Sakai watched her intently now. His wife listened with eyes lowered. Marta couldn't bear to look at the other son. One scornful look would have sealed her lips.

During the movie, she told them as Takashi translated, Noboru didn't miss a thing. When Chaplin tried to eat the shoe, he roared, and then again at the potato dance. When they returned home, he rushed into the kitchen for potatoes and forks and performed the dance for her mother, skipping the potatoes from one end of the dining table to the other.

She didn't tell them how Kino missed it all, how he'd fallen asleep as soon as the house lights went down. How much easier it would be, really, to remember Kino. His astonishment at everything clung to her like a burr. How many times over the years had her mother blurted out at some small remembered thing, "Do you recall when Kinnosuke—?"

There wasn't anything amusing to remember Noboru by. He seldom forgot an instruction, seldom needed to be told anything twice. For him, each new encounter was fixed for life. Not so for Kino. For three weeks, he tackled his new family as if it were a steep and slippery wall that he had to climb again and again each morning.

But the Sakais would not be interested in Kinnosuke. Was it possible to tell them how their son stood out in relief? What could she say? *Your dead son was blessed?*

No. Better to tell the story of the family picnic when Noboru cooked hot dogs, terribly amused by the name, and Kino scorched the buns. Better to say how Noboru had carefully selected gifts to take home, small and boyish things like pens and T-shirts and charms that fitted neatly into his luggage.

Kinnosuke had tormented her mother with two giant boxes of Wheaties that simply wouldn't fit. "Just take one," Mother implored. Even so, Kino's suitcase wouldn't close until Noboru came in and sat on it.

Noboru noticed everything in her brother's room: the baseball pennants and canoe oar on the walls; the large framed celestial map; the telescope in the corner; the *National Geographics;* the books by Defoe and Twain and Edgar Rice Burrows. If Kino had admired anything in Joe's room, he never said, never asked, never as far as she knew took a book off the shelf. Noboru had gone to her mother, *Tarzan* in hand, to ask permission to read.

At just the moments they were most exasperated with Kino—when her father growled and her mother counted to ten—Noboru rushed to his defense. "He's a very serious student, you know." It was even Noboru who took pride in Kino's voice. "His mother taught him the old songs," Noboru had said. "We Japanese greatly admire old folk songs."

It had amazed her how the two boys had moved through their visit, protected by solidarity. At first their solidarity had repelled her, until she saw it again, and lived it fully, in Taiwan. Never alone, except in sleep, Marta moved in a group for nine months. It was like living in a warm cocoon, until one day she thought there was nothing left of her except husk. The boys were not shrunk by their group, they were enlarged. She remembered that now. Even Kino's voice expanded the solidarity of the group, making them all feel proud. But proud of what? Kino? Each other?

Marta finished. Mr. Sakai took a handkerchief and wiped his eyes. Mrs. Sakai's head remained bowed, her feelings held discreetly out of sight. Strange, that Sakai's grief should be so much larger than his wife's. You'd have thought it would be the other way around, unless she was shielding the remaining child. Marta glanced at the other son. For an instant their eyes met, and then he stared into the garden of ferns and stones and bamboo. The reproachful look was gone. In its place she saw something sad and terribly weary.

"Perhaps we could take some pictures," Takashi suggested.

Everyone moved to the narrow veranda. Takashi took his camera, and Marta's, and stepped into the garden while the others arranged themselves in a group. When the pictures were developed, Marta noticed with embarrassment that she was the only one who smiled. It was an American reflex: All family documents should be cheerful. At least she'd kept her lips together. The sight of teeth would have been unbearable.

"That's the statue," Takashi said, pointing, as the car inched past a bald stone figure in a red bib. A wilting spray of flowers lay across its lap.

No one spoke again until they left the neighborhood. Was there anything special, Takashi asked, besides Sakurajima, that Marta would like to see? They hadn't really asked if the trip to the island was something she wanted, but it didn't matter. They drove on in silence until Takashi turned to her again.

"We thought we'd take you out of the city for a while. It's very restful there." Then he smiled. "You did fine, Marta."

Kimura instructed the driver to take them into the countryside, through fields blanketed in yellow rapeseed flowers. They passed a farm-house with a steep tiled roof, then another with eaves of moss-flecked thatch. Perhaps one of these was Kino's childhood farm. Above a field a pair of finches swooped and sang. He was like these birds, really, and the silent, blooming fields. How much he must miss it. It no longer seemed odd that Kino hadn't wanted to tell her. Perhaps he even thought she knew.

The car turned back, and as it joined the deserted coastal highway, she could make out the soft outline of the volcano, rising up from its is-land, calm and vigilant against the sea. For a moment she imagined this place living on inside all those ever born here, even in those who had gone away.

GOODWILL

I was headed for the office when I saw Mr. Her standing between the hedge and the hot brick wall of the apartment. He had his back to me, working a hoe around the same neglected patch of ground he'd been cultivating the first day I laid eyes on him, nearly one year ago. A world of changes had been crammed into this year. For one thing Barbara Spratt had come and gone—come to help the new wives learn "life skills," until she thought she had more to learn than teach, and her heart grew heavy in her chest.

I seldom saw Her during the day, or any of the men. Barbara'd said they attended workshops, learning trades, learning to stuff envelopes with documents. Learning to forget.

I came up to the juniper and looked over. I didn't say anything, only nodded. He nodded back. Plants coiled up out of the ground, running in furrows he'd put there. Seedlings. Earth-hugging vegetables. This year I didn't need to ask what they might be.

Brother Phillip had come himself, paving the way, softening up the boss, Mrs. Sloan. Phil said they were a fine and simple and peace-loving people.

"They love their families," he told us.

"Poppy-growers," said Sloan.

"They just chose the wrong side," Phil said.

"You must mean our side," she snapped.

Sloan usually cottons to every sound Phil makes, but the day he brought in the new people, she turned peevish.

"I don't want any trouble here," she told him. "Willie had to fix up six units, and you couldn't even wait 'til the paint dried before you brought 'em in."

Brother Phillip called them Lao-Hmong. I used to wonder what they called themselves. It wasn't until Barbara Spratt came that I learned the name meant *free*.

The first time I encountered that plot of miracles, I walked right up to Mr. Her. (His backed was turned then too.) I didn't give him any warning, didn't clear my throat or make a noticeable sign. I didn't know then how easy he was to startle. He turned around with that hoe drawn up like a club, his eyes fearful, like some poor beast dogs had chased up a tree.

"Cucumbers?" I'd asked, pointed, smiled. He melted a little and smiled back.

"Pumpkins." It wasn't Her, but a little girl about nine. I hadn't even heard her come.

Both of them were dressed in clothes that might've come from the church basement: khaki trousers held up by a belt; a blue KC Royals T-shirt torn under one arm. They both had on rubber thongs, their feet horn tough.

I looked down at Her's daughter, right into a face as solemn as a rebuke. I felt funny then, like I'd stumbled into someone's parlor where I had no right to be.

I told Mr. Her I was glad to meet him. The girl said something to him, and he made a little bob with his head and body. I made a little bob with mine, and left.

Sloan was just opening up the office when I came up. Inside, the telephone was ringing. I didn't even have a chance to tell her about my encounter with Mr. Her or the garden behind the hedge.

"I swear, Olivia," Sloan said. "They see me coming and just hop on that phone. The sink's plugged. The faucets leak. The hot water ain't hot, and the folks downstairs talk loud all night."

"I'll get the messages," I said and walked over to the answering machine.

She went straight to the coffeepot and cranked it up, opened the windows, ruffled the papers on her desk.

"If you and I had been smart enough to do a little college, way back when," she said, "then you and I might have been able to find something else to do for a living."

"All work's the same in the eyes of the Lord," I said.

"Ha!" The chair squawked as she settled in, bringing in order to start the day. Sloan's a complainer, but she sticks.

"Think good," I tell her. "God don't like ugly."

We're a pair, pepper and salt, both of us hovering near fifty. We each married early on. Widowed early too. Raised our babies and watched them go. Mine come back often—to eat my food and use my bony shoulder. Sloan's lucky if her daughters even phone. My hair's as black as the day I was born, not gray like Sloan's. I have to gorge to keep flesh on, but no amount of dieting seems to change Sloan's pudding shape.

Sloan doesn't live here either, although she could. When I took the job, she told me I was entitled to an apartment.

"The diocese always gives its workers an apartment," she said. "One bedroom."

"I own my own home," I told her. "Airplane bungalow. Detached garage."

Sloan handles the applications, the fancy work. I take the calls, file, or whatever she doesn't want. We both equally hate to type. When Sloan first hired me, she needed a custodian. That changed the second month.

I was in the office one afternoon, doing windows, standing on a ladder three feet off the ground. Sloan was at her desk. A couple of young men she'd been expecting swaggered in. They didn't look like our people. Illegal sublets, I thought. Rough trade from the big Kansas City across state line. I wanted to pick them up with a pair of tongs and carry them out of the room. Sloan was dressing them down for noise, but they had a cold and insolent look. They weren't about to take direction from a short, fat white woman. I came down off the ladder and stood my ground, right behind Sloan, that sharp-looking wiper in my hand.

"You better listen up," I said, fierce as the mama they both ought to have had. "Or you won't be livin' here long."

They laughed, allowed as how I didn't have the power. I fixed on my face a scowl of plaster. "Try us," I said. My son tells me I know how to sound unkind.

After an assortment of manly threats that I knew well enough to ignore, the punks rolled their hips and shoulders on out. I had to tell Sloan I thought she'd won.

When she'd recovered, she said, "Olivia, let's tamper a bit with that job description."

I jotted down the messages, thinking how recorded voices have a tinny sound. Sometimes the voice starts barking right after the beep, and sometimes there's no voice at all. Unused air, like someone holding their breath. I listen real close to the second kind. Like I hear them wondering whether or not they'll be recorded for all time, their gripe preserved and held against them. The corridors were filling up with such strange scents and sounds that the older tenants had begun to feel squeezed out. Put upon, without the history or experience of complaint. The quiet ones never looked for trouble, but trouble was all around. Rumors had been growing like mushrooms in the dark.

Mrs. DaSilva in 204 West wasn't one of the quiet ones. Mrs. DaSilva was a regular caller, mostly because she didn't like to leave the house. When her tomcat disappeared—gone one night, two nights, maybe three—she called to say it was boiling in a Laotian soup pot downstairs. Soon every missing pet became a meal.

"We oughtn't to allow pets," Sloan grumbled.

"One small dog or one cat," I said. "It's allowed."

Four buildings make up the complex, one for each direction of the wind. The office takes up half of East Building's ground floor. There's a courtyard in the middle and a parking lot beside each building. Everyone seems real proud about the off-street parking, even though that's where the trouble first began.

The lots were full of make-do cars, half of them uninsured. Bottom-heavy station wagons, jaded Pontiacs, cars with saggy tailpipes that scraped the pavement whenever they left the lot. When a new blue Datsun arrived in West Lot, it stood out like a fresh-minted silver dollar lying on the ground.

Before long, Mrs. DaSilva was on the phone. She'd seen eight of the new people climbing out of that shiny Datsun. "Eight!" she shouted. Since she was going into the Safeway anyway, she followed them inside. They filled their shopping carts with pounds of rice, institutional-size cans of produce, beans. But it was their behavior at the meat counter that she'd found the most shocking. They argued out loud, "screamed," she said, over worthless knuckles and joints. They'd tried to bargain with a butcher who told them to get lost before he ran behind the paneled glass. Mrs. DaSilva wanted to know what we were going to do about it.

"Do about what?" I asked.

"Those people!"

"I can't do anything about them at the Safeway. Are they doing you any harm?"

"I live here too," she said. "Why, they even hang their laundry out the window!"

I told Sloan about the call.

"I wanna rig a light from DaSilva's apartment to this office," she said. "Whenever she calls, the light comes on, and we'd know not to answer."

"You'll have to answer some time," I told her. "Things are building up. The balance of nations is out of whack."

It came soon enough, in August, sailing through the sultry air of a late Friday afternoon, shattering the windshield of the Datsun. We didn't hear the accident, but we heard the ruckus in the lot—voices raised in a steady, high-pitched wail. We made haste and found a group of new people circling the Datsun. A group of other tenants were talking to a Lao man, Mr. Vang, who was reenacting the accident. Sloan walked up to them, asked what was going on.

"He says someone threw a beer bottle through the windshield." The tenant pointed, and Vang held up the evidence. "Some of them saw it happen from their apartments. Said some people drove by in a big, white car, leaned out and threw the bottle, then drove away fast. He said they were black." The man offered up this last bit like it was a trophy, a bonus. I held myself up tall.

Mr. Vang began talking fast in pidgin: "No like. No like." His hand thumped his chest. A knot of men circled the car. When someone moved aside, I saw Mr. Her sitting in the back seat. Sloan went with Mr. Vang over to the Asians. They let her come. Slow and awkward, she asked one or the other if they would like her to call the police. They shook their heads. "No good . . . No good. No trouble," they said. When she asked who owned the car, Vang indicated they all did.

Throughout the day and into the night, the new men watched their car. Someone told Sloan that Her slept in back. Soon no one wanted to park nearby. Folks began sneaking into other lots, avoiding those watchful eyes. For days all we did was answer the phone, handing out reassurance and advice.

"This one's too big for me," Sloan said and began putting in calls to Brother Phillip. After the third day with no answer, she called the Charities office every hour. She left messages she was sure some secretary was neglecting to pass along. She phoned once more. I heard her.

"If he doesn't come over here today, I'm gone," she shouted into the phone. "You read me? Finished! Kaput! Vamoose!"

Brother Phillip showed up around three. Tall and heavy and dark-haired, he lurched into the office, filling it up, strode over to Sloan, and wrapped her in his big, bear arms.

"Geri, I'm so sorry. How did things come to such a pass?"

Sloan made him a cup of coffee, sat him down, began to tell him how. I made my way quietly toward the door.

". . . And Olivia will back me up, won't you?" Sloan said.

"Yes, I'll do that. When I'm called upon." I left.

I wanted to walk around the complex, read what messages might be hanging in the air. Across the street a school bus stopped. Children tumbled out like candies from a big Whitman box. I saw Mr. Her's daughter cross the street with her playmates—two nougats, one chocolate, three caramels—all of them were laughing to beat the band. I walked around the block to West. Mrs. DaSilva's building. Home of four Lao families, two on the first floor and two on the top.

I let myself into the basement, where we keep the tenants' storage lockers, and the washers and dryers. I went over to look at what the new people might have stored there, but I didn't find so much as a stick. I felt like I was peeking through an empty cell. On the other side, Mrs. DaSilva's locker was crammed with chairs and boxes, black garbage bags with twist ties, and one scarred chest of drawers. Junk. I wondered why she kept it. I'd never keep anything so shameful. I'd have given it away. I went outside.

Since the bottle incident, nobody had been working Her's garden plot. Crabgrass sprouted in his furrows. It made me sad to see it go to weed. The plants were hardy. My hand itched like it does whenever I step into my own garden behind the house. I made sure no one was watching and slipped around the hedge. I pulled up a few large clumps. Then I pulled some more, working the three narrow rows, yanking out weeds like they were a public offense. When the little catch in my back told me I'd done enough, I stood up and looked down into the cold eyes of Her's daughter.

"Your father's going t'have a good crop," I said. "See? Flowers."

She dashed off suddenly, and I didn't know what to think, didn't know what it was about me that made her cease to smile. All I knew was that I shouldn't have trifled.

Brother Phillip had gone by the time I got back. Sloan was on the phone. She gave me a sign with her eyes, mouthed the words *Da-Sil-va*.

"Phil's got someone in mind to come help the new people."

"Help 'em do what? Fortify themselves?" I asked.

"Nothing like that. 'Life skills,' he calls it. Phil says we need to teach them how to fit in."

I hooted. I couldn't stop myself in time.

"What's so funny? It's plain as the nose on your face that something's gotta be done. I told Phil that. I said, 'The balance of nations is out of whack.' He thought that summed it up about right." She looked pleased with herself.

"We're going to have a tenants' meeting. Appoint an ombudsman. Turn this place into an experiment in goodwill."

The words smelled like Brother Phillip. As for me, I'd heard all the stories I ever wanted about Brother Phillip's benevolence. About how he'd taken into his own apartment three Cubans, up from Fort Chaffee, because not even the complex wanted to take the risk. ("The day they move in," Sloan told him, "is the day I quit.") I'd heard all about poor, crazy Emiliano who'd wandered on foot across State Line, past Union Station, down Troost to Linwood, and into a fly-specked dump folks called the Yum-Yum Club. While he was drinking his beer, some drunk stabbed a woman through the thigh. And since Emiliano didn't have the sense to leave, the police took him downtown too: Cubans had been cashing bad checks, beating up on their brethren. Phil had to drive over at midnight to bail him out.

It didn't seem to me that Brother Phillip had done everything he might for Emiliano's "life skills." He'd gone to all the trouble of finding Emiliano a job and a house and a church right here in Kansas. He might have at least warned him about Missouri.

Brother Phillip put the office chairs in a circle. Mrs. DaSilva sat between Mrs. Garcia and Brother Phillip. Mrs. Wade from 112N, between Phillip and Mrs. Tomasic from 311N. I sat between an empty chair and Sloan. We juggled coffee mugs too hot for our hands. It was a pitiful small group, and the only black face was mine.

Why hadn't Sloan, or Phil, called up Celeste Jordan over in 201 East? The problem was Celeste was hardly visible. She worked long hours at the Med Center, and when she wasn't working, she was busy raising kids. Good kids, doing well in school.

Sloan was more likely to think of Nadie Johnson than she ever was of Celeste. I tried to see it in my mind: Sloan in Nadie's parlor in 203 East. Sloan, tripping over five active children under eight, bright ribbons in their Rasta hair; Nadie, in her hair rollers and fluffy mules—the same mules and rollers she wears to the Safeway; Nadie, smoothing a tacky red housedress over that hillock of a bottom; Nadie, like a cinder block, opening the door to Sloan: "Whatchu waant?"

Twenty-five minutes after we're scheduled to start, a young man arrived, wearing a coat and tie. He said his name was Pao. He didn't speak English well, but said what he had to say with great conviction: "Too much of us. Bad feeling. Very bad."

Mrs. DaSilva and Mrs. Wade nodded. Brother Phillip clasped his hands together and leaned forward, while I held my breath, waiting for the moment when DaSilva would start up. Phil took charge.

"We're a nation of helpers," he said. "Of Good Samaritans. Now we're called upon to help again."

"Must be 'cause we're so good at helping the ones already here," I said.

"Sometime or other, we all need a second chance," he said.

"I know that's right!" I said. I was thinking about Nadie, but Sloan was giving me a gloomy look.

Phil suggested that Sloan work with the older tenants, and someone new would come and introduce the new wives to local customs: how to carry out the trash in Hefty bags, how to cover up the food in plasticware and store it in the fridge, how to use the Kenmore washers in the basement.

"I have the perfect person in mind," Phil told us after the others had left. "I think you'll find her highly suitable. She's a recent widow with a great deal of time on her hands."

"Olivia and me are widows, and we don't have a bit of time," said Sloan. "Are you doing this for her health or mine?"

"Trust me, Geri."

A picture of Nadie Johnson floated through my mind. Nadie ought to find herself a turban, a floor-length skirt, a floaty Ethiopian dress.

"She's here," I said. "She's at the curb now, waitin' for traffic to clear."

I pointed out the window. Sloan got up to look.

The woman was pushing back a piece of yellow hair that kept falling across her eyes. She couldn't have been much younger than me or Sloan, but she was a good deal better preserved. She had on a crisp, blue blouse with a high collar and a pleated white skirt. A thin woman, with thin eyebrows and too much lipstick and rouge. I thought of a great blue heron, landing in the office door.

"Mrs. Sloan?" she said, in a voice plump as a feather pillow. Then I smelled her, heavy and sweet. I'd never much cared for store-bought scents.

"I'm Barbara Spratt. Brother Phillip Giraud called me the other day—you know Brother Phillip, of course—and he said to me, 'Barbara,

I have a job for you, a job that's just going begging and needs your helping hands. I have some ladies from faraway Laos that I'd like you to take
under your wing . . .' "

I didn't know folks still talked like this, outside of pamphlets and
books. I lost the words soon enough, listening to that voice patter on
and on, building up steam like a kettle.

". . . And so I said to myself, 'You must get right on over there this
very day. No more delays. No more excuses. You have to do your
duty, Barbara. You just have to help out . . .' "

"Sit down," Sloan said. "Please."

Sloan busied herself making coffee, waited until Mrs. Spratt had
her mug and was comfortable in her seat, then asked:

"How much do you know about what we need here? What exactly did Brother Phillip tell you?"

It soon became clear that whatever she knew didn't amount to much.

"We could use a little peace and quiet," Sloan said, and I switched
on the answering machine. That was the moment Mrs. Spratt noticed
my presence. The eyes betrayed the smile that dried there on her
mouth. I broke the ice.

"I'm Olivia Bledsoe. Mrs. Sloan's assistant. We are so very happy
you could come to help."

She stared. Maybe my Episcopal voice derailed her, the one I had
learned at my father's knee. No child of Reverend Bledsoe dared speak
up at table without a civil and proper tongue. At breakfast we were
tested on our sums and spelling. At lunch we named the states and capi-
tols. We recited the countries of the world, its rivers and oceans and
lakes. If the sight and sound of me was so unsettling, I wondered what
Mrs. Spratt was going to do with the new ladies in their bright skirts
and head scarves, trilling out their rapid, singsong notes.

Mrs. Spratt needed time to collect herself, so I turned away,
walked over to the files. Sloan was sizing her up.

"Olivia will back me when I say this might not be an easy job."

"Yes," I said hurriedly. "But I do believe you'll find it worthwhile.
And rewarding." I gave her the smile my daughters call the Lord-bless-
us-and-keep-us look. I didn't want it on my conscience that I'd somehow chased her off.

Sloan must have figured that a cold, quick plunge was better than wading in from the shallows. She proposed to take Barbara over to meet Mrs. Her and Mrs. Vang on the top floor of West Building. I offered to cover the desk. They were gone for the better part of an hour. I saw Sloan walk Mrs. Spratt to her car. When she got back, Sloan stood over her desk and hummed.

"Don't hold out," I said. "It's against the rules."

"Why, I do believe you're curious." She chuckled.

"Well, I swan! It's not beneath any human being's dignity to be a little bit curious. But I just can't imagine what that woman could teach another living soul except how to bleach her hair."

"Now, now. Let's not look a gift horse in the mouth."

"Indeed not, but you tell me what you think."

Sloan looked pious. When she spoke, the words fell out like stones. "I think I'll reserve judgment."

"Well, it'll be the first time!"

Sloan laughed, then leaned toward me across the desk.

"She's gonna treat the bugs. She's gonna teach them how to launder their clothes some place other than the bathtub. And she's gonna get the Charities van and haul away all those aluminum cans filling up their rooms." Sloan drew herself up as though she'd seen a historic site.

"You wouldn't believe the cans, Olivia. Boxes of 'em, bags of 'em. Some just lined up along the wall. 'Cans for cash,' she told them. 'We'll sell 'em,' she says. 'They probably need the money.' It was like she had a plan, a vision, right after she walked through Mrs. Vang's door."

"And did the ladies understand a word she said?"

"Don't know, but the children understood just fine. You'd have been impressed, Olivia. She was real polite. They gave us some little dessert to eat. I didn't like the look of it, but Barbara ate hers, right down to the last gooey crumb. But I tell you, she cast her eyes on those cans and it was like she'd found new meaning. Like she was thinking, 'I have a dream—' "

"Those are fine words!" I said, loud and hot. "Don't you squander them!"

Sloan's face went slack, and I felt a thin green mist seep up around my anger.

"I think I'll call it a day," I said and took my pocketbook out of the file drawer. "I'll be in bright and early in the morning."

"Suit yourself," Sloan said.

I opened the office at 7:55 the next morning. Sloan arrived at 8:05. Mrs. Spratt walked in at 8:15, fresh as a daisy. The phone was already ringing.

"Coffee?" Sloan asked her, but she said no.

"I have so much to do, Mrs. Sloan. Today we organize the cans. I phoned Brother Phillip yesterday, and he said we could have the van tomorrow."

She had a box of garbage bags under her arm.

"I'll just go on over. Mrs. Vang's expecting me."

True to her word, a driver brought the van around the following morning. From the office window, I saw Barbara, Mrs. Vang, Mrs. Her, and three children squeeze into that bag-filled van. The children must've sat in their laps.

Three hours later they came back. Barbara brought the women and children into the office. Before they returned, it seems, the women and their cash had been parted at the K-Mart. They'd bought yards of colorful remnants: bolt-ends of hot pink polyester, a yard of turquoise cotton broadcloth, green gingham, blue calico, and orange terrycloth. The women were very proud.

"A fire sale?" Sloan asked, shading her eyes, but the colors cheered me right up.

"I think they're interested in texture as well as color," Barbara said.

"I hope so," Sloan said. She hadn't budged from behind that wall of a desk. I don't believe Sloan sewed. I couldn't imagine her ever passing a fabric counter just to run her fingers through the cloth.

When they'd left, Sloan turned to me and said, "Did you get a load of that chartreuse piece? Lord have mercy, what's it for?"

Laundry was a different matter. Throughout the fall, clothing draped the open windows until I thought Mrs. DaSilva was going to ring the phone off the wall. When Barbara Spratt asked if the women knew how to use the washers, Sloan said she didn't know.

"Perhaps a demonstration is in order," I said.

"You're right!" said Sloan. "Olivia will show you the way."

I followed Spratt, who was marching across the courtyard like she was seventeen, me puffing in the rear. I stayed out in the hall while Spratt explained herself with her hands. By the time she'd finished, a group of other women and children had gathered round. She led the group to the basement with a pile of soiled clothes. The children fairly danced down those stairs, like they were going to a circus.

I opened the basement door. The women didn't seem to realize that their apartment keys opened the basement too. When I told Barbara, she said cheerfully, "I don't believe they even lock their doors."

"Well, you tell them they should," I said, real gruff. "You lock yours, don't you?"

She drew back, eyes wide. She scared easy, like Mr. Her.

I stood off to the side. Barbara opened the washer lid, closed it, opened it again as if the women had never handled a hinged surface. As if they never opened and closed the doors of the communal blue Datsun. As if lids didn't exist in Laos.

Spratt sprinkled laundry powder in the machine and invited each lady to observe the blue granules at the bottom. Finally she added the clothes.

"Balance, ladies, balance," she said. "The load must be evenly distributed . . ." She took the clothes out and put them all back in, in thirds around the stem.

Her demonstration wasn't having the intended effect. The women were singsonging fast and furious, and the children were beginning to giggle. A child's voice piped up in English.

"No, no, Batty. Cost money." The girl pointed to the coin slot—$.50. "Upstairs okay. Free."

Even in the dead of winter, skirts and towels and T-shirts flew from open windows, like multicolored signals of distress. Families must have been turning up the heat to counteract the chill. When Sloan read the December gas bills, she shrieked and pounded the top of her desk.

"This has gotta stop!"

Barbara showed up on Wednesday, and Sloan spelled it out: she'd have to charge the families more rent if they kept the windows open. I looked up but held my tongue. Sloan had no authority to raise rent. Unused to Sloan's hard, spiky words, Barbara looked as though Sloan had threatened her with bodily harm. All she said was, "Oh, dear." She turned around—she'd never even taken off her coat—and walked out of the building.

"That was mean," I said.

"Yeah, but let's see if it works."

I would've liked to have been a fly on the wall. It was early, children still in school. Who was there to tell the ladies what she'd said? What kind of pantomime could Spratt perform, what words would plead her case? What did they know about the cold that ravaged us on the Plains? I knew Barbara had already brought them socks and lace-up shoes. She'd caught some children running through a December snow, wearing those blasted rubber thongs.

"Olivia, will you stop pacing? You're making me nervous."

"Then give me something to do."

"I'm not your nanny. I've never had to find things for you before. Something's on your mind."

"There's not a thing on my mind except my empty hands."

"You pace every time you're waitin' for a problem to take shape. Then you talk my goddam arm off. Spill it. I'm growing old just waitin'."

"I'm not worried. I'm just pondering. How's Spratt going to tell those women to stop drying laundry out windows? For all we know, that's what the open windows are for."

The phone rang, and Sloan answered. I took my coat and left, walked over to my car, opened the trunk, and pulled out a bundle of hangers I'd been collecting for the church.

I knocked on Mrs. Vang's door, but Mrs. Her answered. I heard Barbara's voice coming from the bathroom. I followed Mrs. Her inside.

"All the clothes can go here," she was saying, but the women were talking just as fast. She threw a skirt over the shower rod, took it down, threw it back over.

"Mrs. Spratt?" I said from the hall. "Give them these. They'll get more drying space for their dollar."

She turned and stared like I'd walked out of the wall. Her eyes fastened on the hangers, and she gave me a sunburst of a smile. "Oh, Olivia! You're a godsend."

I was suddenly surrounded by smiling women, saying things only the good Lord could understand.

"They'd like you to have some tea and rice," Barbara said.

"No, thanks. I had breakfast."

"It might be nice to take it."

I felt ashamed. I knew better. I let Mrs. Vang lead me back into the living room, where she sat me on a couch. It gave me the chance to look around, since I hadn't noticed much when I walked in. I was too intent on reaching Barbara. There was the couch I was on, an ottoman, and a huge television set on a rickety metal stand. At the other end of the long room were a rectangular table and six mismatched chairs, two of them intended for a porch. I couldn't see the kitchen. I didn't want to. On one living room wall was a big calendar with a picture of some Oriental movie star. That was all. I hadn't even peeked into the bedrooms.

The tea didn't taste like anything I'd ever drunk. They gave me a little plate with a square of white substance that Barbara called "sweet rice." I didn't let myself think too long before I took a bite. It was sweet, all right. Sticky, corn syrup sweet. I ate two more bites to be polite. "Even if it's hateful, always take three." My mother's words. Three for the Blessed Trinity.

Barbara had been working with the women for several months, and I didn't know the smallest thing about what went on. I'd taken in her reports with half an ear, with a little "un-huh, un-huh, that's nice."

"How much do they understand?" I asked Barbara.

She gave a little shrug, a dainty movement, hitching up her shoulders a quarter of an inch, her face turned away like a girl.

"Bits and pieces. Of course, the children do quite well."

I left, finally, and the women walked me to the door. When I turned to say good-bye, I saw they had every intention of seeing me down the hall and stairs and out the building.

When I made it outside, I felt as if I'd bust loose from a corset, the way I'd felt as a girl, leaving the close, dark homes of my father's elderly parishioners. I used to go calling with my mother, sitting in overheated parlors, perched on red velvet settees with crocheted antimacassars, doilies, and milk-glass lamps on the end tables. I didn't understand how Mama had endured it, even though she did it every week and reported she liked it fine. Maybe liking wasn't the point when it was something that had to be done. Anyway, after the hangers, Barbara and I got on just fine.

A week passed before I realized what Barbara had achieved. I'd been looking across the courtyard when my inner eye told me something familiar was missing. I was taking a message off the machine and it struck me: Nothing, not even a scarf, was hanging out a window.

"Look there!" I shouted. "Just look at the landscape!"

Sloan whirled around in her chair, squinted, turned back.

"Don't see a thing," she mumbled.

"That's just it. She's gone and done it. They're all drying their clothes inside."

Sloan's chair screeched as she swung it back around. She pushed herself up and out and came over to the window, looked from building to building and then back to West.

"I'll be damned," she whispered. "And how long has that poor woman been trying?"

When Barbara stopped in later that week, Sloan was waiting with a face full of smiles. A picture, it was. She actually got up from her desk and welcomed Barbara at the door. This so surprised Barbara, her eyes and mouth formed three *o*'s. "Congratulations," Sloan said. "This is a day to remember. How'd you do it?"

"Do what?" she asked.

" 'Do what?' she says." Sloan turned to me, her face clowning. "I'll tell you what. Getting those people to stop hanging their clothes out the windows. That's what!" Sloan thumped her on the shoulder.

"They have?" she said. "I'm so glad." I could barely hear her voice.

Sloan called Brother Phillip to report Barbara's success. After she'd talked with him, she turned to me, slapping her small hands against those stout thighs.

"Phil has the best idea. A little party for the tenants."

"I didn't know there was a clubhouse," I said dryly. The idea had an unwholesome feel. Who was going to type up the announcement and send it around?

Sloan got Willie to clean up the basement of West. Saturday morning, she and I festooned it with crêpe paper and balloons. Willie carried down a long collapsible table and two dozen folding chairs, loaned to us from the Charities office. Sloan got a twenty dollar contribution so we could have cookies and punch.

At 1:00 P.M., Mrs. Wade brought down an old record player that sounded like it was regrooving the surface of her records. Since word had gotten out about the party, some teenagers with a rock and roll band carried in a microphone and amplifier, and performed for a circle of admiring children. The kids danced round and round, when they weren't pressed up close to the guitar player. I spotted Her's daughter among the new kids. I asked Sloan three times whether she'd told Barbara about the party.

"Stop fussing, Olivia. 'Course I told her."

The Lao ladies arrived en masse, without a single husband, loaded down with noodle dishes and that sweet sticky rice. I'd never seen them so dressed up, their bodies clothed in long, bright skirts, heads wrapped in matching turbans. Mrs. Vang came up to Sloan and asked, "Batty here?" I took my place behind the punch bowl, filling paper cups.

Barbara didn't arrive 'til close to four, just as the junior band was finishing a number. All the children were jumping and shaking, their mothers sitting in chairs along the basement wall. I watched Her's daughter move her little stick body to the rhythm of the rock, like she'd been doing it all her life. Three of Nadie Johnson's kids were there, although I couldn't find Nadie. I stared out across the dancers to the door and saw Barbara, standing like a stranger who'd wandered in off the street. I waved her in, and Sloan launched herself off a folding chair.

"Welcome and howdy," said Sloan. "Glad you made it. I's beginning to think you'd forgotten us."

Mrs. Vang and Mrs. Her spied her and rushed over, each one on an arm. They led her to a chair. Mrs. Vang gave a quick little command to a child, who appeared with a cup of punch, another child with a plate of noodles and rice. They hovered over Barbara like hens.

Barbara began saying something to them, gesturing, moving her body in an imitation of a dance. Her's daughter appeared with a record and put it on that scratchy player, everybody talking at once. Barbara said something to Sloan who nodded and came to the front and spread out her arms.

"I got something to say," she announced. "Our new tenants would like to perform some dances. Let's give 'em a hand." She clapped while the other tenants joined in halfheartedly.

The women and children lined up. As the record started, with its drum and piping music, they began to sway and move in parallel lines, then into a circle. Toddlers followed in their mothers' steps. Mrs. Vang came up to Barbara and Sloan and took their hands, pulling them into the circle. Some of the teenagers joined in for kicks, laughing, making faces, and every child, except Mrs. DaSilva's, had joined in almost as soon as the music began.

Mrs. Her came up to Mrs. DaSilva and invited her with a smile. DaSilva shook her head, waved her hands back and forth, then laughed out loud. She pushed her daughter toward the group, but the little girl clung to her mother's neck. DaSilva's boy, a small, jolly kid, joined instead. By this time half the room was swaying or pretending to sway to that fluted faraway music.

When the record stopped, the Lao ladies bowed to everyone around them. I clapped along with the others, including Mrs. DaSilva. Then before I could stop her, Sloan was on her feet again, announcing in a voice like a roustabout that I was a singer, a soloist in my church choir, and wouldn't everyone like to encourage Olivia to come on up and perform a couple of spirituals? I wanted to drown her in a tub.

"You want this party to end in a hurry, don't you?" I whispered.

The Laotians were watching Barbara. When she clapped, they clapped too. I left my position behind the table and came round to the front, but it didn't seem right.

"Go on, Olivia," Sloan said.

"It's been a long time since I sang a cappella," I said.

"Give it your best shot," said Sloan.

I folded my hands, closed my eyes, shutting out the audience as if it were a firing squad. " 'Sometimes I feel like a motherless child,' " I sang, slow and mournful, like it was intended. When I opened my eyes later, the basement had thinned. I caught a glimpse of some teenagers creeping out the door. Mrs. DaSilva had gone home with her brood.

The Lao ladies and children were sitting quietly, watching, their faces blank. For a moment I thought I'd done something wrong. When I finished, Mrs. Vang rushed up to me and clasped my arm, her round, unwrinkled face looking up into mine. I took it kindly that they'd been listening so hard they didn't even clap. Barbara came up and said, "That was simply lovely."

"And didn't you like the dances?" Barbara asked.

"Mrs. Her's daughter was one of the best dancers," said Sloan. "Did you see her, Barbara? Jiving to beat the band."

"I had something else in mind," she said.

"Why, I thought those little Asian kids were just as good as those black kids. Whose children were those, Olivia?"

"Nadie Johnson's," I said and looked at her hard. "You do remember Nadie, don't you?"

Most everyone was gone. Sloan picked up the push broom and began sweeping up the leavings.

"I was thinking about the Lao dances," Barbara said in a disappointed voice. "I thought how much more beautiful they were, than all that rock and roll. I don't understand why we always have to leave things at the lowest common denominator."

Sloan stopped sweeping, for the broom handle had suddenly leaped up and clattered to the floor. She looked at Barbara, whose own gaze was elevated, thoughtful.

"I don't think I understand. I thought all the children were having a good time. Like they were supposed to."

"But why do we have to encourage them to dance like *that*?"

"Because they were in the basement of the Highland Apartments, Kansas City, Kansas, U.S.A. That's why. What do you expect them to do?"

"It's us, Mrs. Sloan." Her eyes seized on something grand, something Sloan couldn't see at all. "We must help them to maintain themselves, don't you see?"

"No, I don't see. They're doing a swell job of maintaining, all by themselves."

"Do you know what my next project is?"

"No. Surprise me." Again Sloan pushed the broom.

"Have you seen any of their handiwork?"

"Of course. They used to hang it out the windows."

"Didn't you notice their skirts and scarves? They also make little pieces that would be beautiful as wall hangings or ties. Just think how good this would be for them. They need the money."

"Don't we all."

Sloan maneuvered the broom around a corner, Barbara following along beside. I collected the empty cups.

"I know it would work," Barbara said. "It's only a matter of finding the right approach."

Barbara started coming in every day to see about the cloth. She
had the ladies digging into boxes and drawers, pulling out finished and
unfinished work.

"I tell them how Americans love hanging things on wall," she said
cheerfully. "I thought they might be able to sell on consignment. I'm
going to contact the Ethnique Boutique downtown."

Some mornings she arrived with shopping bags full of thin balsa
dowels and bias tape, then left for the day, empty-handed. She liked to
stop in before and after she'd visited the ladies, report her progress or its
lack. They were having trouble with the bias tape, she said. They
couldn't get the knack, couldn't see how the dowels would slip
through the tape if only they'd sew it across the bottom and the top.
The women kept buying orange and turquoise, instead of beige. The
tape disappeared into the body of the cloth, became a border, or a
figure, or a lake. They kept working on panels worth hundreds, she
said, instead of nice little squares worth tens. How on earth were the
women going to make any money?

Over the course of several weeks she began to look a bit tired. I
noticed a sag along her shoulders, as though she were drawing their
puzzlement deep inside herself. Sloan didn't take much notice, but I
did, especially after she'd brought in the cloth.

"It isn't fair to say these people have no written language," Barbara
told me. "See, Olivia? It's only hidden, here, in the cloth. The pictures,
there. This embroidered symbol. The women all know how to read
the pictures. They know exactly what they mean. I'm the only one
who doesn't know."

You'd have thought that in not knowing she'd somehow let them
down.

She brought out a stack of large, square panels and explained the village scenes: the harvest celebration, the baby's birth, the valuable horse in
a tiny corral, the barnyard ducks, the men returning from a forest hunt.
The picture panels were bright and strong, each one a different story.

From the bottom of the pile, Barbara pulled out one last cloth
made up of orange and yellow splashes. A river of blue velvet ran across

it, separating one figure from a group. In the upper right corner, a gray silk airplane rained down silver-threaded bullets.

"When I saw this cloth," she said, "I thought I was seeing Moses, fleeing with the Israelite children."

I drew a breath and felt my heart beat hard. I looked up finally and into Barbara's eyes. I felt like I was meeting her afresh.

"I asked them what it meant," she went on. "The women didn't say anything, only giggled, if that's what you'd call it. Then I asked one of the children what it meant. The girl just looked at the floor and said, 'I was only a baby then.' "

Barbara folded up the disturbing cloth and tucked it away.

"I have eyes," she whispered. "I shouldn't have asked."

"You didn't mean any harm," I said, but I don't believe she was listening.

Barbara stopped coming to the office before going to Mrs. Vang's. Some mornings we'd see her crossing the courtyard. Other times we'd only see her when she was getting into her car. I missed those regular reports.

We were about to the close the office one Friday when Mrs. Vang appeared. She smiled at us, speaking real slow.

"Monday, you come? Batty, you, come my house. Party?"

I cut Sloan off before she could pronounce some objection or denial. I said we'd be happy to come. I nodded my head up and down in agreement, and she left, pleased.

"What the hell was that all about?" Sloan said. "Who's Batty?"

"I'll go to the party if you don't want to. I figure she's talking about Barbara."

Sloan and I sat on the sofa. Barbara was on the ottoman, the women and children scattered around the floor. I thought Barbara looked a little frayed. Mrs. Vang came out with a package wrapped in tissue and set it carefully, reverently, on Barbara's knee. Barbara folded back each leaf of paper until she reached the skirt. Tears sprang into her eyes. The women began to nudge each other, laugh, until Barbara was laughing too. Sloan hadn't touched her plate of rice. I jabbed her arm, leaned over while everyone was watching Barbara and whispered, "Take three bites."

Sloan and I left soon, so Barbara could do her work. After the skirt, it seemed like a private affair, and no one was minding the office.

Barbara stopped in late the next morning, looking like she hadn't slept a wink. She was wearing the new skirt.

"I've learned the most wonderful things!" she said, putting her bags on the floor. She pulled out a square of intricate, stitched fabric. "They call it *Pa Ndau!* . . . Flower cloth."

She brought it up to Sloan's desk and laid it down. "Look here. Cross-stitch, appliqué, embroidery . . . and here, batik."

She dove into the bag again and again, taking out rolls of cloth, unrolling them across the desk. The three of us leaned over the pile. Barbara picked up a large square, like a scarf.

"A woman probably made this cloth to carry her new baby on her back. But here's the thing. The borders! Dragon scales and snails and elephant feet. They're for protection. They keep the good spirits in and the bad ones out . . . Oh! I ask you, Olivia. Wouldn't you love to stitch a moment in your life and keep it safe with elephant feet!"

"And your skirt?" I asked.

"My skirt?" She looked down, then back up with a feverish brightness in her eye, laughing louder than I'd ever heard her laugh. She pulled the hem up slightly, running her fingers along the white appliquéd border.

"How silly of me! I didn't even notice it until now. It's the eight-pointed star. For good luck!" She fairly shouted.

"I'll be at Mrs. Vang's a while," she said and left.

Sloan and I looked at each other, bereft of words, as though they'd been stolen from our mouths. We moved slowly through our chores, quiet as country mice. Not a sound passed between us until it was three o'clock, when Sloan said, "Let's call it a day."

I spent a troubled night, and then a troubled week. When I got to work each morning, I felt the lock turn hard against my fingers, felt each file and surface as though my skin were overripe. The air I breathed came in short and shallow. By Thursday, we hadn't seen hide nor hair of Barbara Spratt.

"Where's Barbara?" I asked Sloan, as if it were a casual thing.

"Don't know. I was havin' the same thought."

By Friday morning I could hardly bear the thought that I hadn't been a bit of help, to anyone. I was flipping through files when I remembered the downtown store where Barbara was going to sell the Laotian cloth. On consignment. I phoned and talked to a young woman who sounded as if the store only handled the Crown Jewels. She said, yes, a Mrs. Spratt had inquired about selling some Laotian handiwork, had nearly pestered her to death. "But you see," she told me, "we don't sell froufrou." When I asked her if she'd ever seen any of the handiwork, she said, no, she hadn't. She didn't have the time.

"That's a pity," I said, thanked her, and hung up.

About ten, Willie rushed in, so worked up that his glasses had steamed.

"She be over there, Miz Sloan. Over at the new people's. That be her car in West Lot. I couldn't figure it at first, that strange car. Someone visitin', I thought. Then she called me direct to come over right away and fix a toilet. Don't know how she got my number."

"How long's she been there?" Sloan asked.

"All week, ma'am."

Sloan and I vacated the office like we'd lost twenty years. We followed Willie across the courtyard to the entrance of West, where he stopped short.

"I ain't goin' in there again. She be a sight."

Sloan nodded, making sure, at least, that I was close behind.

We hestitated at Mrs. Vang's door, then Sloan knocked hard. One of the little children answered. We could see Barbara on the ottoman, sewing something she held in her lap. Mrs. Vang came to greet us, and Barbara looked up, smiled as if we'd been expected.

"We're finishing up several of these wall hangings," she said, like she was picking up a conversation we'd been having just a little while ago. "Mrs. Vang might have a buyer for her skirt. To the tune of several hundred dollars! Isn't that grand! If we can just get all these finished, we'll have enough for a special show by Easter. But I'm having a little trouble with the tape."

She got up then, brought over a square of fabric to show us. She was sewing a length of bias tape along the top.

"See? This is what they can't get the hang of. And tell me, how can I possibly reproach them?"

"Where've you been staying, Barbara?" Sloan asked.

"Why, right here. On the couch."

Mrs. Vang wanted us to come sit down. And so we sat, since we hadn't thought what else to do. One of the other women slipped into the kitchen—for tea, I guessed—and Barbara followed her in. Barbara moved funny, like she was pulling her body through a pool of oil. The back of her skirt was as creased as slept-in skin. When she came back into the room, I saw the grease spots down the front.

"I called that boutique place downtown," I whispered to Sloan. "She did contact them, but they turned her down."

Barbara came back in and sat on the ottoman. A toddler crawled into her lap. Mrs. Vang brought us each a cup of tea which we accepted, smiling like a pair of Sunday-only worshippers. Inside I felt my heart slip down. Barbara spoke to the child, then said something about the tape to Mrs. Vang.

"I'm calling for help," Sloan said.

Sloan left, telling Barbara and the ladies that she had to return to the office. I sat where I was, listening to Barbara, watching her close. So much stitching going on. Time moved slow, and I wondered if my watch was stuck. When I couldn't stand it any longer, I asked if I might do a little sewing.

"That would be grand!" Barbara said.

She cut me off a length of tape, handed me needle and thread, and a large square cloth. A little boy crawled up beside me, watching me with marveling eyes, as if I was something from a foreign planet. I longed to touch his sweet, brown cheek.

I turned the hanging over to see what'd been embroidered there. Two identical trees balanced each side. Red and yellow birds and white-faced monkeys perched on the circular branches. Below the trees, deer grazed beside a silken lake. I heard an ocean of blood pounding in my ears. My hand draw back, unwilling to put a single hole into that garden. I turned the cloth back over, quick, making stitches so small no one would ever know they were there.

I was knotting my thread, cutting it with my teeth, when I caught sight of Sloan. Brother Phillip stood just behind, his kind face a mask of dread.

"How good of you," Barbara said to him. "Did you come to see our latest project?"

The room of eyes became one eye, measuring each step. Only Barbara seemed to pay him little heed.

"No, Barbara. I've come to take you home."

There was a long silence before she looked at him, direct, and then I saw that she'd been waiting for this all along.

"How thoughtful of you, Brother Phillip. I won't be a minute. I think Mrs. Vang is getting the knack."

She turned to the women, took both of Mrs. Vang's small hands in hers. "Have faith, dear. All this beautiful cloth. We'll find a home for it yet." Brother Phillip took her arm.

"Do you know how long it takes to make one of these skirts?" she asked him.

"No, I couldn't even guess." His voice was soft and low.

Barbara's hand brushed the creased and spotted skirt, then up to touch the uncombed hair. They walked slowly down the stairs, Sloan and me behind. When she reached the landing, Barbara stopped as if she'd been going up a flight of stairs instead of down. Mrs. Her and Mrs. Vang waved from the apartment door.

"Bye, Batty," they called until, faintly, her hand barely moving, she waved back.

"Brother Phillip?" she said. "Did you know it takes a woman a year to make one of these skirts? . . . Isn't that something?"

We left the building and walked into the courtyard. Sparrows chirped and flitted.

"Will you look at that?" Sloan said, staring up.

Mrs. Her and Mrs. Vang, their children and their friends had reappeared, waving from the apartment windows, the doorway, the landing.

"What d'ya suppose—?"

"Be still, Geri. Let them pay their respects."

I believe that every woman and child would have stood there until day turned to night, if that's how long it took Brother Phillip to cross the courtyard, holding Barbara's hand.

A Novella

THE CLAY THAT BREATHES

THE CLAY THAT BREATHES

1

Eve had thought about Donald Furey at supper and into the final evening hours aboard ship, until he entered her dreams that night: He was walking through a deep exhibition hall, surrounded by student work, picking up a plate here, a vase there, stooping before a black sculpted amphora as heavy as stone. Around him stood clay columns, massive as uncut Venetian marble; coiled terra-cotta jars; surreal painted heads; a giant clay hand, each finger mounted with a smaller hand, waving. "I'll be here when you get back," he said. "It's a life sentence, you know."

Eve was awakened by a shrill of sea birds, then some commotion in the narrow space between the passenger cabins. All sea motion had stopped.

From deck to gangway to dry land, sharp, impersonal Japanese elbows urged her along. The men around her all seemed to speak in low, gruff bursts that made her ill at ease. By the time she reached customs, she felt completely out of sorts, unable to take in anything except the crowd. She was waiting for the official to clear her luggage when she caught sight of a small man with pure white hair, propped up

on an ebony cane. He was standing straight ahead of her, well beyond
the narrow rows of tables, cluttered with open suitcases. The old man's
western suit hung over his body as though he'd recently shrunk. Passen-
gers clustered in front of the examination tables, pressed forward into
queues, the queues pressing on toward a great sea of people who waited
at the far end of the pier, but the elderly man was clearly alone. He
sorted through the crowd that continued to disembark from the
Ryukyu Maru, until his eyes rested on Eve. Wada-sensei. She hadn't
expected anyone. Her Japanese wasn't good enough.

The week before her departure, she'd phoned her teacher Donald
Furey in a panic. What was she to do when she stepped off the boat?
Who was she to see? For the first time since she was a child she felt utterly insubstantial. Was she the same person who had left her parents'
comfortable Michigan home, buoyed by their support and her own
sturdy conviction? For two months she'd shared her sister's cramped
Seattle apartment, studying Japanese at the Seattle Public Library, making arrangements to take a ship from there to Kobe. Not once had she
doubted herself or the purpose of her trip, until that final week. Donald
tried to subdue her fears, advised her to phone Wada-sensei after she'd
arrived and settled in. Wada would help her find a suitable potter.
Donald had already given her a letter of introduction, but she was
unprepared for this.

Eve stared back, into the dark eyes that had already found her. The
whiteness of the old man's hair astonished her.

The elderly man approached. "Eve Sandler?"

She nodded. He handed her a business card, one side of which was
printed in English. *Wada Katsuichi. Ceramist. Retired.*

"What arrangements have you made?"

"None." She had meant to say that she planned to phone several
recommended places, that she was not lost, or forlorn.

"None? Then you must come with me."

Wada pointed with his cane. She picked up her suitcases—her
trunk would be fetched later, Wada said. He led her away from the
pier, out into the harsh light of day.

"In here, please." Again, the pointed cane. She entered the back
seat of a small black limousine that was waiting ceremoniously at the
curb nearest the entrance to the pier. White, laced antimacassars

covered the back and arms of the cushions. Wada got in beside her, said something to the driver, and they left the wharf at Kobe.

"How is Professor Donald Furey?" he asked at last.

"He was fine, when I last saw him. He was preparing a student show. An exhibit."

"He was a driven man, your teacher. Did he ever marry?"

"Oh, yes. He has a daughter now. And an infant son."

"Good. . . good."

"You knew him in Canada, then?"

Wada nodded. "Yes. Didn't he tell you? I came as a visiting . . . what do you say? Lecturer?"

"Yes, of course. He spoke highly of you." She reached for her handbag to get the letter of introduction, but Wada put out his arm.

"He wrote," he said.

"I'm sorry. He didn't tell me. I feel very unprepared."

Donald hadn't even told her that Wada spoke English, and she said so. Wada laughed.

"And how do you suppose I could lecture at Donald Furey's university?"

Eve smiled. The car ran parallel to the harbor for a time, and she saw briefly the *Ryukyu Maru*, placid in its berth. The curved and busy harbor stretched out beyond the ship, taking on a grayer blue than the sky. Its width astounded her. From the water she hadn't noticed its crescent shape. Through the opposite car window she could make out the city rising steeply, up and up, as though Kobe were a series of stairs, a thin terrace of streets hanging on a cliff. At first, close to the wharf, the city seemed undefined, another "international port," a jumble of English, Russian, French, and Italian signs amongst the Japanese. She could no longer smell the pungent, fishy Inland Sea, only the faint scent of upholstery and cleanser.

"You're very young, aren't you," Wada said. "But Donald said you had promise."

Embarrassed, she said nothing. She'd always assumed that what Donald appreciated was her assistance in the ceramics studio. Drone work. Hoisting bags of clay. Supervising underclassmen. Cleaning up. How often she'd felt like a burro, saddled with water jars and firewood. When she had finished her degree, Donald arranged for her to stay on

with a small grant. In exchange for her help, he let her use the studio
after hours, gave her a discount, fired her work with the others.

"We shall see," Wada said. "Anyway, Donald seemed concerned.
And since he took care of me, you see. While I was a visitor . . . But
you will have to learn a little of our difficult language, I'm afraid."

Wada turned and looked at her directly, the first time since they'd
entered the car. What must he see, besides a girl in a jeans jacket, jeans,
and hiking boots? Something shapeless, hopelessly young? She stared at
her boots—swollen things, utterly incongruous with the car, the doilies,
Wada.

The drive to Kyoto took nearly two hours, through dense, tangled
traffic. There had been nothing to see, nothing to take in, except the
highway—the concrete road, concrete abutments, guardrails and cars
and masses of overhead wires. The context was both so foreign and so
familiar that she felt dazed by the time they stopped in front of a small,
walled home. They entered through a tall wood gate, took five steps
across a manicured garden of pebbles and stones, into the house itself.
Above the low entry, the floor of the house was elevated by at least two
feet. In her haste to remove the boots, the laces knotted. She would
have cried were it not for the sudden appearance of a small, gray-haired
woman in a black kimono, who dropped to her knees in one swift
move that took Eve's breath away.

With the solemnity appropriate to a church service, Wada-sensei
introduced her to his wife, Hiroko-san, and disappeared, as if swallowed by the house. The two women stood alone. The silence lasted
only a moment before Wada's wife waved her in, smiling, speaking in a
sweet, lilting, encouraging voice, as though Eve understood each Japanese word perfectly. Hiroko-san spoke no English whatsoever.

Eve had her own small six-mat room at the Wadas'. She thought at
first it must have belonged to one of their children, but they had no
children. Wada-sensei said that his mother had lived in it, long ago.
The furnishings consisted of one low table and a single light fixture that
hung from the shallow ceiling. A window overlooked the sheltered garden, and a soft pearly light filtered through paper panes. Sliding closets
were built into the wall. Here she laid out her jeans, blouses, sweaters,
her one skirt and dress.

She eagerly wrote to her family and her friends. Later, and with more care, she wrote to Donald. "Can you imagine? I'm living in Wada-sensei's home!" How would Donald cope with a life lived on the floor? She saw him perched on his favorite stool, dressed in his flannel shirts, sleeves rolled up, faded jeans flecked white with dried clay. Would anyone call Donald *sensei*, looking as he did?

Flamboyant Donald, whose own work was exhibited widely and sold well, who became more outraged, and outrageous, with each success. She was always puzzled by his attitude, as though his success were an unwelcome guest. He was one of the stars of the department. His work was featured in other ceramists' books. His pale blue and celadon glazes were envied and imitated. Although Donald did very little work of his own on the wheel, he promoted its use and was considered a desirable teacher. Nowadays he worked in large, often rectangular, decorative bowls. "Suitable for a flower arrangement," he used to say. He approached an angle with the seriousness that the Chinese had once approached a curve.

He kept one pale Ming vase—a gift from a different Japanese ceramist—inside a display case in his office. When students brought him work he considered inadequate or showy, Donald would turn to the Ming vase, and say, *Let this be your teacher. It was probably made by an illiterate fifteen year old boy, whose hands shaped dozens of these each day.*

What a contradictory man Donald was! Yet because of Donald Furey she was a potter, not a watercolorist or oil painter. She had taken his introductory course in ceramics. Optional fare, lumped carelessly with sculpture. The third dimension came to her with the force of a conversion. In his loud, earnest voice Donald told them stories of famous potters and potteries, taught them shapes and elements and glazes, filled them with the history of the craft. It made her smile to think of it. Donald was at his best with the introductory classes, the innocents, unaware of the extraordinary love they were about to receive.

Eve, too, was smitten. Here was a medium with a life unlike any other. She was astounded by its texture, its elasticity, and weight. The feel of a clay shape was reassuring in a way a stick of charcoal or a brush could never be. She began to spend her free time in the University ceramics studio, until she became a fixture, a knowledgeable and reliable assistant, an "old hand."

When Donald had last summoned her to help him set up a student show, he had alarmed her by disparaging the exhibit. "Why is it," he'd said, "that one cannot be small and good at the same time?" He pointed down the imposing line of student work. Not one teacup or salad bowl or salt shaker. She'd thought he was being perverse. Couldn't he see how much his opinion and approval mattered? Why would any student try to win Donald's respect with a garden shed of a pot?

"Go away, Eve. Branch out. Grow. Unless you leave, you'll never realize how little you know. What you *don't* need is to come into this studio every day and see bad work."

In the months that followed, his words had returned again and again, even here, seated on the *tatami* of her new room.

In and out. Up and down. Eve followed Wada's wife, Hiroko-san, from kitchen to bath, from laundry to garden. Eve left her shoes in the *genkan* and would never dream of slapping anything but bare feet against *tatami*. She folded and unfolded bedding, aired the futon each morning, beat it clean. She watched the old woman closely, imitating as best she could. Each of Hiroko-san's gestures in the house, every greeting on the street was instantaneous, intuited, as automatic as breathing. Chores and meals bulged with lessons.

"Would you like to come to the market?" The old woman stood in the entry of Eve's room, dressed in a gray, tightly-patterned kimono. She had been living with the Wadas for three weeks.

"*Hai,*" she answered. Yes, she would love to go. Eve closed her Japanese language text and felt the tightness of her jeans against her thighs. She would have to change first, and pointed to her legs, muttering *jeans* and *no good*.

"Oh, it doesn't matter." The old woman said and smiled. "All the young women wear jeans nowadays."

"*Chotto matte kudasai,*" Eve said carefully. "It'll just take me a moment."

Before they left the house, Hiroko-san handed her a plastic shopping bag. Eve had stopped at the market several times during solitary walks or returning from the language school, but she had never before been asked by Hiroko-san to accompany her.

They followed the narrow street north for a block, before turning onto an adjoining road that wove down a sharp hill to the neighborhood market. Houses stood close to the street, their privacy preserved by weathered wood walls. Occasionally, a hinged wooden door stood open, and she could gaze into an entryway or garden or even up into a parlor. Preschoolers played in the street, unconcerned with bikes and motorbikes or cars. No sidewalks here, only the street and covered sewer that ran beside it.

They hadn't gone far when they were stopped by a woman of Hiroko-san's age who greeted them with a deep bow and enquired about the sensei. Another acquaintance passed, and then another. With this third, once the greeting had completed its great slow arc, the old woman introduced Eve as the "disciple" of one of Sensei's colleagues in the States. The woman smiled at Eve, nodded, spoke some pleasantry or approval that transcended Eve's understanding.

There was something reverential in all the greetings, and each woman had inquired about the sensei. Even in retirement, he was treated as a gift to the neighborhood, an asset, and by association, his wife as well. Eve would never have guessed this. The Wadas' house was no larger than their neighbors. The clothing they wore bespoke humility, not fame. As they continued their journey to the market, Eve felt too tall, too blond, utterly out of place. At least she'd changed into her dress.

She had been with them six weeks when the old woman was stricken with a sick headache. "It's nothing," she told Eve, and took to her bed. Eve persuaded her, in her fledgling Japanese, to send her to the market instead. Eve thought she wouldn't have agreed if Sensei had been in the house. Had he been there, the old woman would have lifted the compact hoop of her body out of her sickbed and made him tea or brushed his suit. Yes, Eve could go, but only after Hiroko-san had given elaborate instructions in her most patient Japanese, while lying down—Eve poised on her heels, pencil and paper in hand.

You must go to Yamaguchi-san for radish and spinach but not the beans. Go to the man at the far corner stall for beans . . . Buy only 200 grams of stew beef . . . Visit Inoue-san for dinner tofu, and whatever you do, child, don't buy the pebbled, brown-flecked fried tofu . . . Be sure to examine the eggplant in Nakamura's pickle vat for signs of age and imperfection.

Eve felt light-headed by the time she had finished taking down the directions. When she returned from the market, the old woman examined each purchase and then, smiling, patted her hand.

Only when the term finished at the language school did Sensei begin to speak of an apprenticeship for her. Eve had hoped that she might work with him, and told him so, somewhat bluntly, she realized too late. He laughed. "Ah, but I am now retired, you see."

Students of long standing and trust—sons to him almost—had taken over his responsibilities at the pottery, and on three occasions he took her there. When they arrived, Wada was treated with such deference that she came to see why he did not visit more often. All activity stopped. Even those women hired to wash up went down on their knees. During the first visit, Eve was shown where clay was processed. The second time, the wheel room and the kiln. The third, the room where potters applied decoration and glazes.

Sensei said little during these tours, and when each visit was over, Eve left the pottery in a strange taut state: she was as unformed as the clay being slapped and wedged against the wooden work table. She had always thought that the task before her involved only herself. But the pottery was crowded with workers: not just potters but cleaners and scrubbers and sweepers. It was not at all as she had imagined, a room with one potter and his wheel. Still nothing fundamental had changed. More than ever she felt like the child who'd stayed home too long. After the third visit she told him, "I want to begin."

The waiting continued. She wrote to Donald. "What do I do with my hands?" ("Whatever you can," he wrote back.) She turned to sketching, a childhood pastime, the filler of hours. Hiroko-san found her in the front room, drawing the iris and vase that stood in the *tokonoma* alcove. "Wait one moment," she said, when Eve had finished.

The old woman went into Sensei's study and returned with paper, ink and brushes, placing them on the low wood table where Eve had been sketching. From then on, whenever Eve was home in the evening, the old woman brought out the rice paper and brush box.

As Eve rubbed the ink against the stone, gripped the brush, poised it over thin paper, her heart shrank. The road to calligraphy was as tortuous as the road to clay. She was a child again, learning penmanship. A child of seven, times three.

With each new character, Wada's wife came around the table and gripped Eve's hand in hers, so that Eve might "feel" the character, so she might achieve the proper state of tension in tranquility when the strokes were made. "*Kimochi-ii*," she crooned.

But Eve could not forget her legs that had fallen asleep, the tiny pinpricks of recirculated blood, the cramped forefinger, her shame at each blotch because she'd made the ink too thin.

"You will learn," the old woman said. "It all takes time, and children here start so young."

On the way to his study, Sensi stopped once to watch. "A valuable skill, Eve-san. Wherever you go, you will need to use the brush." Sensei's approval altered the pleasantness of this pastime, bringing with it the weight of obligation.

Enough of all this time! The juice of her life was spilling. She was no longer a child, and all she ever wanted to do was pot. Smother her hands and clothing in clay. Knead and smack and wedge. Dip and stir. Guard the fire in the kiln until it reached white heat.

Eve had been with them six months when Sensei brought her into his study. He seemed unusually serious, as solemn as the first day he'd brought her to the house. He opened the sliding door to the closet behind his desk and removed a balsa box, the size of a shoebox, wrapped in pale blue string. Inside was a *sake* bottle and three tiny cups. Unpretentious stoneware. An earthy beige with a faint rose blush along the shoulder of the bottle, another blush along the lip. The decoration, brushed on, was of some kind of grass she couldn't identify: a plume of four leaves out of which sprang two tasseled stocks. Lotus? Rice? Miscanthus?

"They came from a small pottery," Wada said. "Everyday ware, mostly, although Oita's father and grandfather made ceremonial jars. For personal use."

Although she had traveled with Wada to several kilns, she had never known the nature of the negotiations. Nor was she sure whether Oita's pottery was one of those they had visited. Perhaps Oita was the only potter who would take her. Perhaps being a foreigner and a woman counted as three strikes.

Eve picked up the small bottle. It was pleasant to hold and fit perfectly into the curve of her hand. Wada made no further comments while she examined the stoneware. When she put it down on his table, he carefully replaced it in the satin-lined box and returned it to the closet.

"Do you like it?"

"Yes."

"Good. You might learn a great deal here. And what you would learn with Oita could be carried away."

The old woman refused to leave the kitchen. They heard her crying as the luggage was carried out to the front of the house. Sensei grew impatient: the car was waiting. He might have stopped her tears with one privileged male bark—Come out! But Eve had never heard Wada raise his voice to his wife in the six months she had slept on their floor and eaten their food, all her fears of Japanese men preempted. The Wadas were bound together in far more than years. It was the formality of this marriage, its great dignity and weight. He did not, would not, command her.

"Go to her, Eve-san. She's too kindhearted."

And so Eve went, and would have put her arms around Hiroko-san, except for that immense ceremonial shield that guarded every thought and gesture. The old woman still would not leave the kitchen, even after Eve promised to return soon, to spend with them whatever holiday she could eke out. Hiroko-san wiped her eyes on the edge of her immaculate white apron.

"What would Sensei say!" she said in her teasing voice. " 'Silly old woman.' I'll just stay right here. Don't forget your lunches. It's a long drive . . . Make sure Sensei wears his scarf."

They traveled south, into the industrial quarter of Kyoto and out again, onto the provincial highway, turning east toward Mie. With patience, the driver navigated through turbulent waves of private cars, buses, delivery vans, through schools of tiny darting scooters. When they reached the countryside, the road snaked down into narrow cultivated valleys and up again, through steep wild hills of bamboo and rhododendron and pine.

"Remember, Eve-san," Sensei said, his eyes fixed to the back of the driver's head. "Nothing important is learned in less than ten years.

You will be with Oita one, two, perhaps three years. A short time, so learn what you can."

She listened reverently, the way women here were supposed to listen.

"Give this gift to Oita's wife." He reached down to the car floor and brought up a package wrapped in silky, pale blue paper. "You must help her, you know. You're an intruder in her home."

"I thought I'd be earning my keep by helping him."

"How? You're worthless to him now, but not to her. And you must be careful not to hurt her feelings. With the clay, you belong to Oita. In the house, you belong to his wife."

2

At first, she was always in the house.

"When you clean the table, please use the blue cloth," Oita's wife Makiko explained in rapid Japanese. "Not the white one. The white one is for cleaning the knives. The yellow one is for washing the dishes. Please remember, Eve-san. Don't be so careless."

There was nothing affectionate about Makiko's instructions, or perhaps it was only hidden by the peevish edge in her voice. But then Makiko was so much younger than Hiroko-san. Thirty-five, Eve guessed. On the day that Eve and Wada-sensei had arrived, Makiko's greeting was as correct and formal as Wada's wife's had been, but what had followed was utterly cool. Perhaps the greeting had only been meant for Wada.

Did you clean out the bath, Eve-san? No? Would you do it, please. The last person always does it . . . Are the oshiboris ready, Eve-san? No? They must be piping hot by the time Oita comes back . . . We Japanese don't boil the water for green tea. It scalds the leaves, makes it bitter. Foreigners never understand about green tea . . .

Learning to rub ink and hold a brush were heavenly pleasures compared with this. People here were always finding new ways to complicate their lives. After one especially trying morning in the kitchen, making eggplant and cucumber pickles, Eve teased Makiko that houses in Japan were difficult to live in. She hadn't meant to be taken seriously. Perhaps she'd chosen the wrong verb, for Makiko took the words to heart. For days on end, Eve could do nothing right. Makiko was everywhere at once, to correct her and watch her and complain.

When Eve's kitchen work was finished, or when she'd done what little she was allowed to do with Oita at the pottery, she helped the grandmother—Oita's mother—in the garden. It was a good chore, with weedless tidy rows, and no dish cloths.

"Do you see this bug?" Obaasan asked. "The cabbage is disappearing because this bug eats so much."

"Why don't we spray it?" Eve asked.

"Oh, no, no, no! Here we do everything by hand. No sprays. Only the best for our family. We kill it this way—pinch it between your finger and thumbnail. Just snap! See? But we have to do it every day. The cabbage is beginning to look like Oita's old underwear." She laughed, covering her mouth with her hand. "Here. You hoe and I'll pinch."

"But you have to stoop. Let me."

"Oh, no trouble. I'm closer to the ground anyway. Watch today. I'll let you pinch tomorrow."

Tomorrow. What was this tomorrow that stretched in front of her like an uninhabited land?

Indoors, she found Oita's two older daughters sitting near their mother. Yoko, the baby, was in Makiko's lap. The infant still cried whenever Eve came near. She heard Makiko coo, encouraging the baby.

"Bashful, Yoko-chan? Are you bashful?"

"Here, Oita-san," Eve said in a hearty voice and offered to take the child. "I have two little brothers at home."

The baby screamed, arched her body away from Eve and clung to her mother. Makiko smiled. Nanchiko, the oldest, laughed and chanted: "Yoko-chan, Yoko-chan! Yoko's afraid of the foreigner!"

She turned away and busied herself at the sink. It was incredible, the ease with which the little girls used that word. She'd once thought the word was merely descriptive.

The two older girls were sent outside to the grandmother. Makiko attached the baby to her back and began her dinner preparations.

Something else troubled her about little Nanchiko besides the chanting. Eve singled her out for attention, as if this might lessen the tiresome pipe of her voice, her sulks, her alarm at everything sudden or new.

The girls did not seem like children, but miniaturized adults—spotless, clean-handed, constrained from anything that might soil them or the house. Even the baby was in training, and would be free of diapers, Makiko said, before her small feet touched the floor. Did any of them have a scratch or a bruise? So far, they'd never allowed Eve close enough to for her to tell.

She remembered the rambunctious tone of her own family, with its two girls and two younger boys. How they fought, and she with them, the daily territorial battles which progressed, with age, from name calling to sabotage to temporary teasing thefts. If there was any such cruelty among these children, it was kept well below the surface, exorcised at infancy, each child pampered in turn, the breast given to Yoko the baby whenever she so much as murmured. The sweetness of it all! Except to her, the outsider, the *gaijin*.

The kitchen door stood open. Eve could make out the top of Nanchiko's head above a row of eggplant. Suddenly, Nanchiko released a cry that trailed off into a laugh.

"Okaasan," the girl called.

"Hai, Hai," Makiko answered, her voice sweet, available. Nanchiko ran toward the kitchen, her arm outstretched, stopping just beyond the clean and sacred boundary of the house. She held up a notched, chartreuse worm.

Alarmed by the competing voice, the baby clung to Makiko, fussed.

"Okaasan," Nanchiko called again. "Look!"

"Not here," said Makiko. "Take it back."

"But Obaasan said it's eating everything in sight!"

Makiko stomped her foot, a small ineffective stomp, more a symbol of annoyance than a threat. The very same stomp the older girls gave to Makiko, and each other.

"Nanchiko-chan! Please!"

"Show me," Eve said and stepped outside. Nanchiko thrust out the writhing worm and Eve took it.

"A beautiful specimen! Show me where you found it."

"Obaasan said not to bring it back."

"Let's take it out to the field."

The little girl stopped, frowned.

"There'll be lots of things for it to eat there, you know. Maybe even some relatives. Come on."

Eve strode along the edge of the garden, the worm in the cup of her hand, past the shallow fence row toward the meadow beyond. She heard the little girl running along behind.

"May I have it back, please?"

"Of course. Here. Hold it carefully so it won't get an upset stomach."

Nanchiko giggled. Funny that these children weren't afraid of insects, only dirt. They walked on together until the little girl stopped abruptly.

"I can't go any farther," she said.

"Why not?"

"Mother says so. It's not safe."

So much fear. Was it any wonder? With every fourth step Makiko called out to them in her sweet, cautioning voice, *abunai, abunai.* "It's dangerous!"

"All right," Eve said. "Let's look right here for a place."

The girl took a few steps back, a step to the left, to the right, peering through weeds and grass.

"Do you think it's a mother?"

"Probably."

"Then we have to find a special place."

The child began to move back toward the family compound, stopping ten yards outside. "I think here."

Miscanthus grew thick against the side of a small green hump. One thorny shrub struggled beside it. Nanchiko parted the grass carefully at the base of the shrub and placed the worm in the depression.

"There! We mustn't walk here now."

"Of course not. We'll remember the little tree." Eve pulled at the shrub. "We'll walk around."

Nanchiko clapped her hands and dashed toward the house, calling her mother.

What would she do with three small girls? She remembered her own mother as a disciplinarian, with a commanding voice. Makiko's voice wouldn't have cut the mustard at their house. And when they were bad, Mother had sent all of them out to the weeping willow that grew at the back fence. "Cut a switch!" she had told them.

She had never seen Makiko lay a hand on these girls. Sweetness, everywhere. Even in moments of irritation. Where did the anger go? And the girls, so dependent on Makiko, far beyond what you would expect of the age: Nanchiko, six; Fumiko, four. The attention paid these children was extraordinary, as though the rearing of children were a social contract, each one born to be reared the same: coddled, stuffed as infants, taught beyond a shadow of an error, so that they might be suitable occupants of the fragile wood and paper and *tatami* houses. Safe in the elegant little kimonos they wore. And such a show by the mothers. Their sweet instructional voices sang on and on in the background, instructional Muzak that accompanied the children wherever they might be. *Here I am. Be careful. "Abunai."*

Her own mother would have viewed such sweetness with a jaundiced eye: one must never spoil the child. Eve wondered if she'd been watched as carefully as these girls were. She couldn't recall now, although she remembered how they had played in neighboring yards and alleys. Did boys here get the same treatment? In this household, she'd never know.

"Cut a switch!" said Mother. "Two feet at least!"

★

Inside, Eve and Makiko moved silently through their dinner chores until Eve couldn't bear it any longer.

The night before, she'd heard Oita arguing with his wife. As soon as Eve had stepped into the bath, they'd started up—shouts and whines coming from the kitchen. Then he hit Makiko, once, and the sound chilled her, right through the hot water. Eve had stayed in the *o-furo* longer than usual, sunk deep in the tub. If she had left, she would have had to cross the kitchen to her room.

Eve hesitated a moment, her fingers straining wet rice.

"Did your husband hurt you last night?" she asked quietly, half expecting, half hoping to be ordered from the kitchen. To her surprise, Makiko answered.

"Sometimes a man must hit his wife," she said and dropped seaweed into boiling stock. "It just shows I wasn't being a good wife. It can't be helped, that's all."

Eve couldn't bring herself to look at Makiko. Oita's advice sounded so far away: "Concentration, control, and peace of mind. Without these, Eve-san, you are not ready to throw a pot."

She had begun to think she'd never be ready.

She felt best out-of-doors. Had there been no garden, no grandmother, she wondered if she might have left, written Wada and Donald and announced her resignation: *I am not fit for this*.

She'd arrived at the Oitas' in early August, just before O-Bon. Now, in the false spring of October, Obaasan planted turnips, burdock, great long *daikon* radishes, moving through the garden like a small purposeful beetle, bent and clean and quick. Eve was sent to help. She took the hoe and followed the old woman along the perfect, manicured rows, moving the earth out of shallow trenches onto long smooth mounds. Grandmother moved with such an economy of motion that Eve felt her own great pulling strides to be a form of waste. Perhaps economy was required, when you lived on an island, where nothing could be lost or overlooked. No one moved as fast as a Japanese grandmother, or so close to the ground. Invisible and everywhere at once.

"Where are you going so fast?" Grandmother's coned head appeared from around the leafy knees of a cabbage. Eve heard her laugh.

Eve pulled the dirt back, down one row and into the next. It felt good, this pulling on the earth. Triumphant and flushed with exercise, she rounded the end of the beans and found Oita, waiting.

"Come with me," he said. "There's something you must see."

He called to his mother. "Okaasan, I need Eve-san for a while."

"Bring the hoe," he said.

Eve followed him out of the garden, back further into the property, to the untended meadow. Concealed by tall miscanthus was a small knoll, and beyond the knoll, the clay. She saw a bare spot in a narrow crease of land. Oita strode toward the crease.

"This is our blood. The source. The clay isn't pure, you know. We have to add different elements. But my grandfather was fortunate in this spot. I want you to get the feel of it. It's different from Obaasan's garden."

He pointed. At first she didn't understand what he wanted. She walked to where the earth stood exposed and drove the hoe forcefully into the ground, pulling back a lip of clay. It required more strength than the garden, felt denser, uncultivated.

"Dig a little more," he said.

She chopped and pulled with the hoe. You'd think she was attacking the ground.

"That's enough," he said. "This week you'll help Yamamoto and me dig and prepare."

He left her standing there and walked back to the pottery.

3

Without warning, Oita invited her into the wheel room. She told herself later it must have been her impatience, her gloomy frame of mind that made it seem long. She stood beside him and watched him straighten a spine of clay. A teacup appeared.

"Did you notice how the clay resists?" he said. "It fights back. It has a will of its own. You have to control it, and to control it you must first control yourself and know what it is you are controlling. If you are afraid or if you do not pay attention, the clay will control you. You'll put a hump on its back. Because you do not have as much time, you are starting sooner than most. To master any craft, you know, it takes ten years." He didn't look up. His hands shaped the cup quickly and without hesitation.

Of course, she thought. Ten years for everything.

Yamamoto walked in and nodded to Oita. Whenever he saw Eve, he ducked his head. If she tried to speak to him, he shrugged or went suddenly deaf. Yamamoto had been with Oita three years. He lived somewhere in the nearby village.

Yamamoto made his preparation and sat down at the second wheel, beginning a rhythmical turn of body and hands. Even as he bent across the wheel, he appeared to straighten.

Meanwhile Oita prepared her for the first wheel. He threw the clay, saying it was too much to expect of a beginner to know how to throw it. She didn't remember having any problem when she worked with Donald. Everything she'd learned she had now to learn again, as if the skills she'd brought were fraudulent.

Oita demonstrated the foot rhythm necessary to keep the wheel in motion. Eve sat down and pumped the lever, trying to imitate Yamamoto as she watched him from the corner of her eye. She thrust her hands into the clay which slopped over the wheel.

"Stop!" Oita commanded. "We'll wait for now. Working the clay requires this . . ." He struck his abdomen with a fist. "And this!" He struck his heart. "All you know is this." He bounced his fist off the top of his head.

She watched Yamamoto's hands control the clay. They reminded her of Oita's as they held the mound and pressed with quiet strength until the right shapes magically appeared. Like Oita, he moved in an even, deliberate circle as hands, shoulders, and arms pressed in. When he threw the clay, it landed with a dull smack in the exact center of the wheel, and like Oita, he made it look easy. This was not the same man who'd walked through the door avoiding her eyes, his thin body pulled in like a bug protecting itself against predators. At the wheel, his insect limbs unfolded, growing in size and shape until he looked again like a man, strong and supple.

At the end of the day, Eve followed him to the wash-up sink. Yamamoto bent over the basin and scrubbed his knuckles and nails until the flesh went white. What made him so formidable? A rake of a man and so young-looking, an ageless young, as though the body were stuck at the pupal stage. She'd heard Oita grumbling about his weight.

"Your landlady's cheating you. You're thin as a noodle."

Too much work, Eve thought. Too much trudging from the village and not eating or expecting to eat, finding nothing to savor in it, eating only to live. Eve stood beside him and washed her hands. He didn't look up, absorbed in his cleaning. She turned to speak, but he quickly left the room.

So she had become a listener, an eavesdropper on the conversations between the two men. It bothered her that she and Yamamoto had never had a conversation. She wondered if Yamamoto had a single shred of humor. Around the pottery, he behaved as though all humor had been scooped out, like seeds from a melon.

"Where's Yamamoto from?" she asked Oita.

"Kyushu."

"He's good, isn't he?" Perhaps Oita wasn't in a mood to talk. "I mean, he's becoming good. He seems to have so much talent and skill. I'd be very happy if I could be as good. I feel so awkward in comparison."

"Yes, but that will pass, we hope. Now, please watch."

He picked up a slender tool with a crooked head, like a dentist's pick, scoring the body of the cup. The room was silent, except for the pump of the wheel.

"Why doesn't Yamamoto study with his father?" she asked. She'd been hoarding this tidbit, provided by Makiko during one of their kitchen chats, since Makiko had warmed some in recent weeks.

"Why should he?"

"His father's a potter, isn't he?"

"Yes, but it's difficult sometimes. And you aren't paying attention."

★

How sly Oita was, Eve thought with affection. Step by step, he added one new tool, one new task to the task learned the week, or day, before. By the time the pottery reached its preparations for the spring firing, she'd managed to put away the frustration that had once hounded her. It seemed only natural now—like a kitchen chore—that Oita entrusted her with the unbaked pots. This must be how guildsmen passed along their trade. It thrilled her to think that she could one day say, "This is my life. I do it with my hands."

The kiln was built by his great-grandfather, Oita said. It sat on a steep hill: four rounded chambers stacked one in front of the other down the hill, four brick and earthen humps like miniature Navajo hogans. A fifth chamber at the bottom housed the oven. Heat from the wood fire drifted up the adjoining chambers and baked the clay.

"Watch your head," he warned her. "You have to duck into the kiln. There's an old brick at the entrance to this one, so please watch and don't stumble. Think of all our pots as fragile, newborn children."

"Why don't you just dig the old brick out?" she asked. Oita sighed.

"I like it there. It keeps us all alert."

Oita showed her how to stack the unfired pottery. First her hands, then her entire body grew increasingly alert as one chamber filled and they moved on to the next.

They finished filling the kiln before supper. She walked back to the house as Oita and Yamamoto began bricking up the entrances. The two men worked quickly, yelling back and forth. Suddenly, Yamamoto laughed. She'd never heard him laugh before.

"It's exciting, don't you think?" she said to Makiko as she rinsed the rice.

"What's exciting?'

"Firing the kiln."

"The firing? Why? They're only doing what has to be done."

All she wanted was for someone to share this moment.

"Think of it," Eve countered. "Here are months of hard work. Orders to be filled. Maybe some will break. Which ones? Soon the clay will be fired and . . . who knows what then!" Eve spun around, into a small hopping dance step across the kitchen.

"Yes, but that's the way it always is."

"But your father was a potter. Didn't you ever want to be one?"

Makiko laughed and said something about "how silly."

Then she added, "I suppose I might have once, when I was very young. But it's better work for a man." Eve realized she meant this as a fact and not a judgment.

"You must think I'm peculiar then," Eve said.

"It's not the same for you, is it. You're not like us. Things are different where you're from. Here there's so much else to do besides the pots." A sweep of her hand encircled the kitchen where they stood, the house, garden, work buildings, grandmother, and children—an interwoven universe of obligation. The jubilant mood seeped away.

"Yamamoto is a quiet one," Eve said later. Makiko clucked her tongue.

"A strange one," said Makiko, her voice conspiratorial. "Many helpers come and go, but he's the strangest of the lot. Oita says he's shy, but I don't know. He won't look you in the eye. It's like there's something he's afraid you'll see."

She gave a dramatic shiver and moved to the other end of the kitchen.

"Maybe he's just sensitive," Eve said, as if she had to make things right for him. "An artist's soul, and all that. Oita-san thinks a lot of him, doesn't he?"

"Yes. Oita does."

"Do you suppose Yamamoto resents my being here? He never wants to speak to me."

"Who knows, Eve-san. And if he doesn't like you? Is there anything you can do?" Makiko turned her back to Eve and chopped radishes against a block.

Here it was again, the flourish of resignation.

Sometime during the evening and following day, Oita's friends were scheduled to arrive. Makiko explained that it was a good way for Oita to get together with his colleagues. They'd celebrate the firing, talk shop, and Oita would feel good. Suddenly Makiko's lips trembled. She sniffled. Then the men would drink too much, she said, and spill ashes all over the *tatami*.

Mumbling some excuse, Eve retreated to the garden. She'd never seen Makiko cry, and didn't want to now. The household revolved around Makiko. What would happen if Makiko were removed? In the fresh air, Eve's surprise melted into pity for Makiko, alone, while Oita enjoyed his friends. Did Makiko have friends? There were neighbors, of course, but Eve had seen no friends.

"Was it like this when your husband was living?" she asked Obaasan, who was picking cucumbers for dinner.

"Oh, yes. The same. But louder and better. Friends would come from farther away, take the night train. Oita's father was a loud man. A different man. It was a different time, you know. Men bellowed at their wives." She chuckled at the memory. Eve thought of Wada-sensei, who never bellowed. "I was always so afraid of his voice. Oita is . . . well, a gentler man."

The old woman turned, gasped, "Osamu-san!" and rushed away.

Eve followed her gaze and saw an old man walking slowly up the road that traveled from the village to the Oita family compound. Obaasan ran to the kitchen and spoke to Makiko, who handed her a cloth to wipe her hands. The older woman moved at a remarkable clip out of the compound and down the road. Eve asked who was coming. An old colleague of Oita's father, Makiko said. A retired potter who came once a year to help the son of his deceased friend.

The garden was deserted. A child screamed in the kitchen. Eve hesitated outside the kitchen door, conscious of her faded overalls.

"Come in, please," Makiko called. "I need help." The children were underfoot. Yoko toddled behind her mother, clinging to her dress. Nanchiko teased while Fumiko, the lovely middle daughter with full-moon eyes, watched from a corner.

"Rice? Soup?" Eve asked.

"Yes. Hurry, please." From the open kitchen door Eve saw the grandmother bow to Osamu-san from a distance of ten feet. The small woman bent lower and lower, each time lower than the old man she greeted. The welcome took minutes, threatened to grow interminable, until Obaasan stopped and trotted ahead, turning now and then to encourage Osamu on. The old man moved slowly, and Obaasan arrived first at the kitchen door.

"Quick, Makiko. A towel!" But her daughter-in-law had anticipated her. Makiko reached under the lid of a stove pot and removed a rolled and steamy *oshibori*. Telepathy, Eve thought, from lives so closely lived that Oita's work at the kiln was woven into the fabric of the household.

Osamu reached the front door. Oita's wife greeted him on her knees, while his mother helped Osamu out of his street shoes and into slippers. Their greeting was so elaborate that Eve grew fearful of leaving the kitchen to be introduced. Her verbs could not yet expand in reverence, like the Oita women's. The old man pulled candy out of his pockets. Nanchiko grabbed it all and gave one piece to each younger sister.

"After dinner you may have some more," she said in the singsong voice of her mother.

Some time during the rush, Makiko had pulled back the *fusuma* enclosing another room. Obaasan took Osamu into this enlarged space and insisted that he take a legless seat with a back, an embellishment on the local habits of simplicity and suffering, where families crouched on cushions. Obaasan poured his tea, brought in rice crackers and sliced melon. Nanchiko came in to perform, to sit in "Oji-san's" lap.

Oita finally arrived from the kiln, calling out to Osamu, who responded warmly. Yamamoto had come with Oita. He seldom came to the house. Obaasan the hostess brought more hot towels, more tea and snacks. She coaxed and pampered, making everyone feel snug. So it wasn't Makiko after all who stood at the heart of this family.

The bath was hot, Obaasan announced. After some pulling and tugging, the bathing order was established: Osamu-san must bathe first. The old woman darted into the kitchen.

"Hurry up, Makiko. The men will be starving."

Slowly, Makiko put on her garden shoes and walked outside to a low shrub. Eve watched in amazement. Not just any leaf would do. Makiko reached into the heart of the bush, Yoko dozing on her back. If Eve were Oita's wife, she would have fallen to pieces, utterly dismayed. But the lines on Makiko's face had disappeared. The baby slept undisturbed. It seemed as if Makiko chose to step into the garden at the exact moment she needed peace. Eve followed the movements of this busy woman, her loveliness hidden in an apron. Makiko returned to the house slowly, took the selected leaves and carefully washed each one before putting them into a lacquered bowls.

"Oi! Eve-san. Come here," Oita said loudly. "Bring the *sake* and sit down."

The abruptness of his request made her uneasy. For reassurance, she turned to Makiko who shrugged. Makiko removed a cloth covering a basket of porcelain *sake* cups and, without a word, handed it to Eve.

"*Hayaku,* Eve-san. Hurry up!" In the front room the men laughed, and Makiko sighed as she left.

When the soup lids were lifted, each diner found a single leaf in clear broth. Osamu observed the floating still life in his soup, raised it to his lips and drank. "Eloquent . . . ," the old man whispered. If only Makiko could have heard.

The men were red-faced from drinking when Eve excused herself. Outside, the evening air was damp and cool. She went to the kiln, walked down one side, and up the other to the top again until she heard someone behind her. She turned and faced Yamamoto.

"Are you nervous before a firing?" she asked. He shrugged, stumbled, and leaned against the kiln.

"What did Oita tell you about me?" he asked, his voice husky.

"Not much, that's for sure. Why?"

He only stared at the ground.

"Did he tell you I was foreign?" he asked finally.

"With a name like Yamamoto?" She laughed. "No."

"My grandfather changed it. We're potters for generations. My people brought pottery to this country, and these people . . . these people—." With his open palm, he slapped the old kiln, hard.

"They treat us like dogs. So my grandfather changed our name and married a woman from Kyushu. Do you know why I'm here? So no one will know. My father worries. If I work with him, what will happen? But he's the best. He knows so much about glazes that other men come to him for advice. My great-grandfather kept the old Korean secrets. For generations we've kept them. Still people gossip behind his back, say they don't know him, and then crawl to his kiln for advice. He teaches them what he can. Then they crawl away and say there was an unfortunate odor at the kiln. Like a kennel . . . I know the work of other potters, and my father's work is better. Every year he sends his best work to Tokyo. He never enters an apprentice's work as his own, like some men. But every year the same card comes back with the same official seal. He has never received a national award. There's only one reason. My family has lived in this country for generations, but we're still considered foreign."

"I don't understand," she interrupted. "How can that be?" He didn't seem to hear.

"If Oita's wife knew, do you think she'd allow me to stay? Do you think she'd even serve me tea?"

"She hasn't said anything to me except that your father's a potter."

"She doesn't know."

"And Oita?" she asked.

"Oita? Oita's not like other men. He's my father's friend."

Yamamoto turned and walked away from her, back to the house, wiping his eyes with his sleeve. He stood in the *genkan* and thanked the family, bowed to Osamu, and said good night. Then he left the compound for the village.

Eve didn't want to go back in. She wandered over to the work rooms and went inside. As she passed the wheel room, she thought about what she'd recently asked Oita: "Why did you agree to take me?" They'd been adding spouts to teapots and were busy washing up. Oita had smiled as Eve had seen him smile at the earnest questions of his daughters.

"Why? Because you looked so serious when Wada brought you to visit. As if your life depended on it." He must be teasing, she'd thought. She couldn't remember herself, although she remembered Oita and his respect for Wada-sensei.

"Wada said you were worth my time," he had said.

"Have you taken women apprentices before?"

"Only as assistants, not as apprentices. I thought your presence would be good for everyone. Especially my mother and my wife. I must consider them, you know."

No, she hadn't known.

"A craftsman who ignores his family is a very foolish man," he'd said. She remembered Makiko's kitchen gossip about other pottery families, stories of envy and strife.

"Do all craftsmen consider their wives?" she'd asked.

"I don't know. What I do know is that the world is full of foolish men."

Eve walked up the shallow stairs to the display room and turned on the light. Ceramic tea and *sake* ware sat on dusty shelves, the work of generations, preserved for instruction, reverence, memory. Under the window stood a special group of ceremonial jars and vases. She looked at each, remembering what Oita had begun to teach her in the hours off from the wheel.

"My father used to say that we are not slaves to perfection," Oita had said. "Neither is beauty. Perfection is loud and draws attention to the maker. Even though each of these pieces is exquisitely made, it is still the work of a mortal, not a god. People may be hardworking, pure of heart, even mysterious. But how can they be perfect? No, Eve-san. Fidelity is what you need and what I hope you'll learn. Fidelity is restrained. Only through fidelity will you understand how a pot properly made conceals the maker."

She touched each jar, examining the balance, the shadow of the glaze. Did other potters feel the same, their standards shaped by faithfulness and surrender? Donald seemed so far away now, a man strangely beleaguered by his students' work and by his own fame. Why was it, really, that he had urged her to go away? Some days she thought she glimpsed the reason, and then it would slip away, as her body lurched toward some new task or chore, dragging her mind along.

"If you only want to be an *artiste,* stay here," Donald had said, handing her someone's flashy, amateurish pot. "But if you want discipline? If you want to learn a craft that will never let you down? Then go to Japan . . ." His words grew loud, then blurred as they were overtaken by Oita's voice, murmuring over and over: *concentration, control, peace of mind.*

By the time she reached the last vase, her hands were trembling. Laughter burst out suddenly from the house, and she felt herself grow weak. She sat on the bare wood floor and wept, from the heat and fatigue and despair of what she thought she could never be.

4

Whenever she looked back, the months seemed compressed. Now she worked daily at the wheel. Weeks at it had broadened her shoulders like a swimmer's.

"Repeat work," Donald had called it, but the English words diluted the event somehow, as though sitting hour after hour was some onerous and boring chore, when it wasn't that at all. How would Donald know the unexpected delight of repeat work? The freedom? He lived a life more closely resembling Wada-sensei's. A master potter. A sculptor of clay. Was this the fruition of a career? To be exempt from "repeat work"? Had Donald's training included such long hours at the wheel? He must have said, but that was gone now too, as though the new training had permanently buried the old. As the weeks passed, she felt as though she were turning into rings of sedimentary rock, each raw deposit pressed into a neat and compact layer. What did she owe Donald now? He had never sent her to the edge of a meadow and asked her to dig.

Repeat work. When she asked Oita, his answer was exhilarating in its scorn. *Repetitious? How can it be repetitious! Each pot is different. It has a separate life, takes a separate breath. As unconsciously as you breathe, each one will come into being, or should, if your heart is in it.*

When had everything started working in unison? All she knew was that Oita no longer stood by to remind her to "concentrate, control, and attain peace of mind." She learned to give in when it benefited her most, to clean off the stubborn clay and to start again. Clutter from the kitchen, garden, washroom, and kiln disappeared, leaving a clean and empty landscape.

She looked up from the wheel and found Yamamoto staring at her.

"Look how smoothly you throw it now, Eve-san. *Kimochi-ii!* It's a good feeling, isn't it?"

He turned back to his own work, immediately absorbed as if he'd never looked up at all. She sat still for a moment and bathed herself in this drop of admiration.

When had Yamamoto stopped avoiding her? Both he and Oita seemed less formal, including her in their jokes. It had taken so long to reach this point, as though the first long year were a subtly orchestrated initiation, the burden of worthiness hers alone. But the rite had been so slow and gradual, it was impossible to feel good about the passage. Like congratulating grass because it grew. Nowadays, when Oita wasn't available, Yamamoto—Ryo-san now—offered his advice. *Try this tool, Eve-san. . . Sit this way. Don't twist. . . Why not hold your left hand further up . . .* More and more, he reminded her of Oita.

Perhaps she could ask now, this small, curious thing she'd saved up in her mind, since he no longer shied away whenever she opened her mouth. Weren't they both members of Oita's "guild"?

"Ryo-san, what was your family's name when your ancestors first came?"

Yamamoto jerked up from the wheel.

"Do you know what you're asking?"

His voice was a rough whisper. He got up and cleaned off the fresh clay, leaving the room as if pursued. She could hear him in the distance washing up. How could she have been so blunt? He'd probably forgotten what he'd said. She was sure he'd been a little drunk at the time.

Oita only compounded her misery later the same week. As she helped him prepare a glaze, he sighed loudly and announced that Makiko was pregnant again. Eve congratulated him, wondering why Makiko hadn't told her herself. Oita wandered off, distracted.

"I don't know how this child came to be," he said when he returned. "I've hardly slept with my wife since Yoko was born."

"You've probably just forgotten," she said, stupefied.

"Does a man forget such things? Another mouth isn't what we need."

Ryo-san. Oita. Had they all gone crazy? Oita seemed so dismayed, what would he do? Men here were so strange. Throughout the afternoon Eve looked for signs. She'd read about such things in the newspapers, which seemed to specialize in despondent husbands, abandoned wives.

She half expected to find him sharpening knives. She imagined Oita in a rage drowning Makiko in the bath, cutting out her heart, and finding a blue dishrag. But what would become of Oita? Every headline from every family suicide pact screamed through her mind. *Family of five leaps to death at hot springs resort . . . Mother and children suffocate.*

That night, lying awake in bed, she sifted through the day's debris. Nothing had changed, except her imagination, which had exceeded itself. Oita's air of abstraction was the same as the day Wada first introduced them, when Oita had looked at her and then at the clay between his fingers, in a room full of ceramics as uncluttered as himself.

Meanwhile, Makiko was showing her own signs of stress. Before supper, on a day Nanchiko had whined for candy continually from the moment she got home from school, Eve saw Makiko pinch the little girl's cheek in exasperation. Although she'd thought, in her Western way, that this should have been done long ago, Eve knew it was extraordinary.

To make matters worse, Makiko had reached new heights of silliness in her demands on Obaasan. Day in, day out came a litany of complaints.

Mother, come here . . . Could you reach this for me? Could you pick this up? . . . Mother, I don't feel well . . . I'm so tired, Mother, please hold the baby . . . Eve-san can be so dirty sometimes, don't you think? She never cleans the sink after she's used it . . . Why do you take Eve's side when she isn't even one of us? . . . Please help me, Mother. My back is sore.

The day before Eve's long-scheduled trip to the Wadas', Makiko confronted her, announcing that Eve was being selfish to leave at a time when her help was needed most.

"Why are you telling me this now?" Eve blurted out. Makiko had known of her plans for weeks. "Why is my help suddenly so precious? You've never thought very highly of my help before."

Makiko gasped and refused to speak to her for the rest of the day. Eve felt ashamed, for what she had said wasn't altogether true. But for some time, since the pregnancy was confirmed and the atmosphere in the kitchen had grown tense, she again preferred to help Obaasan in the garden. Still, she was surprised. Wouldn't Makiko enjoy having her own house to herself?

Eve left for the Wadas' anyway, worrying about what mood would greet her when she returned. Throughout her holiday she couldn't free her mind of the Oitas. Wada's wife laughed at her, said she was becoming too serious. With her help, Eve selected gifts for each member of the Oita family, and when she returned, her tiff with Makiko was apparently forgotten.

You look rested, Eve-san . . . How is Sensei? And his kind wife? Did you go anywhere special? . . . You made this sauce? Josu-ne! *How skillful of you!*

Eve resumed work at the wheel, but the memory of Yamamoto's withdrawal, and Oita's startling complaint, returned, disturbing the quiet space around the wheel. Some days she didn't know which distressed her more.

At the last kiln firing, four of Oita's friends had come. She and Yamamoto had joined the potters, and everyone had stayed up late. The men told stories, especially a potter named Matsushita. Matsushita, the storyteller, had pounded her back at the beginning of one evening, then her arm. As the night wore on, the *sake* flowing, he'd startled her by placing a hand on her knee. From across the table she'd watched Yamamoto glare at Matsushita, his eyes two small dark points. She recalled that Yamamoto, in a sudden moment of camaraderie, had whispered to her, "Don't listen to him. He's a frivolous man." It was Matsushita's gaiety and zest that Yamamoto disliked, out of envy.

Mechanically, Eve turned the wheel, unmindful of its pump, listening to the thoughts that clamored in her head like soup lids in the kitchen. She had an image of Matsushita pursuing Makiko. But when? Not during the day. No one was ever alone. A secret tryst in the early morning hours? A rendezvous in the garden after everyone else had gone to bed? The wheel room? No. Makiko seldom came here. She pictured Matsushita moving through layers of Makiko's aprons, coarse kimono, endless yards of undergarments. Then she stopped. Makiko would sooner starve than let his hand touch her flesh. Of this Eve was absolutely sure.

She was misreading everyone. Matsushita was fun-loving, nothing more. Makiko needed Oita as surely as he needed her. She had lived with them so closely, what more could she have missed?

"Eve-san! What are you doing?" Oita yelled. "It's not your job to see how fast the wheel will go! Stop!"

She was stunned. He'd never yelled, hadn't even interrupted her in weeks, and now he stood in the doorway, arms flapping like a madman.

He walked quickly to the wood plank beside her wheel, where they placed the finished work. One-third of the plank was full.

"Look at these! Not one good cup. What are you thinking? What's become of you?"

He picked up the long board, turned it on its end and shook. All the cups fell into a large, moist pile.

"Start again. Pay attention. Remember, please. Control, concentration . . ." He sighed. "And peace of mind."

Eve couldn't bear to look at him. When Yamamoto came into the room, she left without a word.

She rushed upstairs to the display room, her face hot, and stood, motionless, in the middle of the room. She walked slowly to the shelf beneath the windows and touched each vase and jar until she reached the last, her favorite and the oldest. She lifted it carefully, feeling the rough base disappear upwards into the smooth, round body. A low shaft of sunlight struck the jar, illuminating the beauty of the glaze, and she felt the tension drain away.

The men were gone when she returned. Carefully, methodically, she remade the cups she had betrayed and ruined, her mind empty except for a focus on the clay. The wheel turned evenly, and the soft pump of the pedal filled the empty room with muted syllables. "Control, con-trol, con-trol." Her hands and feet behaved as though they had a separate life, as if it were her limbs that told her head how peace was found in work. When she finished, it was well past dinnertime. She walked through the twilight to the house, still free of thought. Makiko was in the kitchen when she entered, and glanced up. She took a cloth-covered plate and put it on the counter.

"Here, Eve-san. You must eat."

★

They were arguing again. Eve could hear them from the bath, sometimes from her room. Oita seemed to be yelling a lot these days. When she heard her own name, she was surprised to hear his voice raised in defense.

"Makiko's pregnancy seems like a dreadful hardship on her, and on my teacher too." She said this to Obaasan when they were alone in the kitchen. The lines of other people's business had blurred long ago. "Isn't there something a woman can do?"

"Of course. You can always do something."

"Does she want this child?" Eve felt the sad weight of Makiko's predicament.

"We want a son."

"We? Obaasan, times have changed. She has three children already. Forgive me, but I heard Oita complaining about another mouth to feed."

"But there is the kiln to consider. A wife must consider these things. As for Oita, he'll come around."

There was metal in the grandmother's voice. Eve had stumbled across some sacred and invisible line, and she rushed ahead to cover up her blunder.

"Do you think so too?"

"Of course. Anyway, Makiko's young and healthy. I'm still able to help. We have a large house. A large garden. She should try."

"But why?" she asked, in disbelief.

"And who do you suppose will look after her when she's reached my age?"

For nearly three years, Obaasan had been a living example, cared for by a son. Yet Eve had been unable to take this in. She had had to ask.

"Eve-san. How do you find my son as a teacher?"

"The very best! He's patient and thorough."

"Ah, yes. And does he only teach you about the clay?"

"No. There are the glazes too."

The old woman smiled and turned away. Alarmed, Eve realized where this was headed and felt as if a fire had scorched her. All this time, she'd thought that what she shared with Obaasan, and the reason they could talk, was their admiration for Oita. When Obaasan turned back, she was no longer smiling.

"I ask because my daughter-in-law believes you are learning more."

Eve stared helplessly at the old woman, outraged now at Makiko's groundless fear.

"Use your head, child. Don't you see what I'm saying? Makiko believes her husband to be, because of you, uninterested in her, shall we say?"

"Why don't you ask Makiko if she's interested in him," she snapped. "I'm sorry. She's wrong. If I'm causing so much unhappiness, perhaps I should leave."

"Now, now, child. You must understand that when a woman is pregnant, she has strange thoughts."

"Only a very special man would take both Yamamoto and me. How could she think he would do anything so common! Why don't you ask him yourself?"

Obaasan laughed lightly, said that wouldn't be necessary.

"What happens if Makiko has another girl?" Eve asked impulsively.

"Oh, I don't think she will."

"How do you know? Did she have a test?"

"Old women know a few things. Makiko is carrying this child differently."

Alone in her small room, it was all Eve could do to straighten the clothes in her trunk. Stung once, stung twice in a single day. Perhaps it was time to go home.

★

The old kiln glowed. Bright orange flames curled out through chinks in the bricked-up doors, although the chambers themselves had long ago turned black.

Matsushita the storyteller returned, but Osamu-san had died in March. Oita missed him and complained sadly that it wasn't the same without Osamu. The old man had always come for the spring firing.

Yamamoto grew sullen after Matsushita's arrival, giving him a wide berth as he carried pots from the storage room to the kiln. Matsushita had brought *sake* to celebrate the firing, forcing it on everyone when they weren't working or watching the kiln. It was mild and sweet, and they drank it cold. Except Yamamoto, who muttered something about an ulcer that wouldn't allow alcohol. It was the first Eve had heard of it. Rebuffed by Yamamoto, Matsushita took to joking with Eve, teasing her with countrified expressions she'd never heard before, until she became uncomfortable. What she couldn't understand seemed full of innuendo, barely concealed scorn. It's only the *sake,* she thought at first, but found herself moving away from him instinctively, like Yamamoto.

Between the heat from the kiln and the humid air, she felt exhausted. They'd worked nonstop until each piece of unfired pottery was carefully stacked, each door bricked up, back and shoulders tense from lifting. When the work was finished, she left the men and went indoors. Only Obaasan remained in the kitchen, tidying up. Makiko was bathing the children as best she could, enormously pregnant, her delivery expected within the month. In her room, Eve pulled out the futon and removed her damp, sooty clothes.

Not even a bath induced sleep. She watched the burning ash of the mosquito coil like a hypnotist's clock, until it dropped into the dish below. Nothing helped. It was too hot, that was all. She tossed the sheet off, dressed, and left the room, moving down the long hall in bare feet. At the kitchen door, she fished out her garden shoes from beneath the step. The air outside felt surprisingly cool, and she walked away from the house toward the pottery. She smelled the wood burning, and the strange, warm scent of clay being baked. Her shoes, slapping against her heels, sounded loud in the quiet compound. Then, in a sudden strong shaft of moonlight, she could see smoke lifting up from the kiln.

A light shone in a second-story window of the workrooms. She couldn't imagine Oita forgetting to turn it off, and she moved across the dark yard like a moth seeking light. Inside, she switched on the entry light, a single dim bulb against the ceiling. Obaasan's frugality, grown into a family habit: nothing bright or wasteful in this unused space. Wearily she climbed the steps to the showroom.

"Ryo-san, what are you doing here?"

Yamamoto turned away from a shelf of vases and faced her. She thought that she'd startled him, hoped even that she had, but he only gave her a long, disinterested look.

"And you?" he asked.

"It's too hot. I couldn't sleep."

"Yes." He turned back to the ceramics beneath the window as if she'd never come in. She would have liked to grab his arm and whirl him around, make him face her while she confessed all the bitterness that had been filling up her heart. Didn't she work here too? Didn't she pull her own weight? *Who, exactly, do you think you are, Ryo-san?* She shrank back instead, closed her eyes, and waited for the anger to pass.

"Which is your favorite?" Eve said finally and walked to where he stood.

"Must I have a favorite?"

"No, but aren't there one or two that draw you somehow?"

He shrugged, and her anger returned.

"How can you be so neutral?" she said. Her voice rose. Yamamoto turned and looked at her.

"Is that what I am? Neutral?"

"That's the way it seems to me."

The room was much hotter than her own. Sweat beaded on her forehead and in the furrows of her throat. She opened a window, then another. They'd had no choice, filling the kiln, except to ignore the unseasonable heat. "Why are you here," she asked, "if there isn't something that makes you come?"

"So many questions, Eve-san. As if there were always an answer, neatly wrapped in a box."

"I'm only interested in what you think. You've been here longer. You've learned more. But you keep hoarding what you know."

"It's Oita-san's job to teach. I'm only an apprentice too."

His modesty irked her. Ridiculous. He was the son of a potter, yet here he stood, unwilling to share the smallest dregs. And why? Out of deference to Oita? She didn't believe it. She had offended him, once, and he'd pulled himself away to punish her. That brief period when he had taken a kinder view toward her had been swallowed up by his grudge.

"What will happen when *you* have an apprentice?" she asked.

"Ah, more questions. How could I possibly know until I have one? Besides, each of us must learn ourselves. It's a matter of feeling. How can anyone teach you how to feel?"

Yes, feeling. The incomparable intuition of the East. He was casting her out again . . . Well, it didn't matter. It was too hot to matter, and he was right. Oita was the teacher, not Ryo-san.

"What if the things I shared were wrong?" he said, unexpectedly.

"I've watched you now for nearly three years, and I don't think that's possible."

"Perhaps I'm not as good as you think."

"Oita thinks you are."

"How do you know? Did he tell you?" He sounded anxious, and she looked at him closely.

"He didn't have to. I can *feel* a few things, you know."

She walked away from him to the opposite windows, stopping in front of the old ceremonial jar. She would never tire of it. She picked it up and felt again the texture of the base as it smoothed into the body of the jar, and in her hands, she could imagine it in its raw, unfired state, perhaps as it might rest on a wheel.

"It isn't a matter of choosing," she said. "It's just that I feel something special with this one. As though everything that needs to be learned and cherished can be found here, in this one pot." She put it down and turned toward him. He was smiling.

"So, you're beginning to read the clay, just as Oita said you would."

"Whatever that means."

"Come with me. I want to show you something."

He headed for the stairs, and she followed, down into the shipping room at the back, where orders were packed and sent. He pointed to a bench beside the worktable.

"Here. Sit down."

For how many months now had she been doing what she was told? He disappeared then, reappearing suddenly from the shadowed hallway, something small in his hand. He sat down beside her on the bench, and she became aware of the dimness of the room, so far from the house. He kept his hands, and whatever they held, on his knees, under the lip of the table. He seemed ready to bring it out when he sighed and stopped.

"Last night I had a dream," he said finally. "You were in it too . . . We were being chased. Both of us. I recognized some people like Matsushita, who doesn't like me, and Oita's wife. There were others too, with sticks and shovels and hoes. Before they reach us, we jump into the kiln together. We were firing it, like now. The kiln burns for days. Even after they stop putting in wood, it burns. It's us. We make it burn, somehow.

"When the fire finally stops and the kiln is cold, Oita takes out the pottery. It's all black, but not ruined. More like glazed marble. Exquisite and smooth . . . A kiln full of jet black jars. No one will touch them. Except Oita. Then I wake up. I know then that you and I . . . that somehow we're one and the same."

One and the same? She couldn't have heard him right. She must have pulled back, unaware of moving, for now he was reaching toward her, with a look of urgency that transformed his face into a grim mask, until the only thought her mind could hold was the thought that he was mad.

"No, Eve-san. Please!" Something fell under the table and broke. He clasped her hands, and for one moment she saw them standing at the oven door, prepared to leap into the fiery kiln of his dream. "There's something else—"

She jerked away, swatted his hands, her legs tangling in the bench as she stumbled to her feet. Then she was running, out of the room, down the dim hall, across the dark compound to the house.

5

Slippers scuffed along the hall. A door slid open with a muted breath, letting in a sharp arrow of light. The light was quenched, and a voice from the belly of a drum whispered, receded, spoke again from far away in the house. A breeze stirred through the dust-dry room. A window must have been opened, but when? Obaasan wouldn't be pleased—a window left wide. Obaasan believed in thieves in the night.

Whatever it was, this thing attached to her swollen head, it felt as unfamiliar and heavy as a lead-filled sack, thrown across the floor. Her eyes wouldn't open, as though rusted shut. She was drifting again and wondered, strangely detached, whether it was possible to faint while already asleep.

The susurrous feet returned, stopping somewhere nearby. A shadowy, sweet-smelling shape drifted down, then hung over her, round as a balloon. The stubbled cloth laid against her head might have been a brick, and then it softened against her skin, the coolness seeping in.

A different, more sibilant voice whispered, "How is she?"

"Fever. We need some ice, and a fresh towel."

"But she has her clothes on!"

"Yes. It must have hit suddenly."

"I'll help you take them off."

"In a moment, Makiko. Let's bring the fever down first."

She became aware of the clothes, wrapped tight like a second skin. She wanted to speak, but the sound that pushed up out of her throat was dry. Her lips repeated the words until a murmur came out. *I'm sorry.*

"Hush, child. It doesn't matter. Makiko is bringing aspirin."

Obaasan held her head while she took the pill, holding the glass steady until one, two, three sips were taken down, and she drifted off once more. She was barely conscious of time, only of the voices and heat that came and went in diminishing waves. The fever subsided on the third day. When she awoke, she was conscious of feeling light and free.

Obaasan appeared with bowls of *miso* soup, chicken broth, rice, black tea. She didn't know how often the sheets covering the futon had been changed and washed. When she was able to sit up for any period of time, the old woman took the bedding and hung it over the bamboo pole outside, beating it, leaving it there to air.

By the end of the fifth day, she felt restless and decided she must go to the pottery, for an hour at least. Now she should offer her help in the kitchen.

She stood up, and the memory of the night she'd returned in frightened haste lurched out, buckling her legs. She didn't know what she would say, or do, when she saw Yamamoto. If simply remembering her behavior made her swoon with shame, what effect would the man himself have? He was explaining a dream, that was all. In the last few nights she had been visited by dreams equally frightening, like sharp fragments of brightly colored glass.

Oita was alone in the workrooms. She could see him at the back, taking chemicals out of the glaze storage jars: flint, whiting, china clay, feldspar. She knew the contents of each jar by heart, and could have found them in the dark. She took her apron off the hook. Yamamoto's apron was gone, but she couldn't see or hear him. She walked over to where Oita stood, his back to her.

"May I help?"

At her voice, he turned around and smiled.

"Well, well. You had us all worried."

"I'm sorry."

"Nothing to be sorry about. It takes a long time to build up strength for this work. Especially if you weren't born into it."

He stirred the contents of the bowl with a thin wood paddle.

"Ryo's gone home," he said matter-of-factly. "He said he didn't have a chance to tell you. What with your illness."

He wiped his hands on his apron. She felt a chill, and when it passed, relief.

"When's he coming back?"

"He's not. His father wrote. He's needed there now."

The rooms seemed unnaturally empty and still.

"Was he ready to go?"

"That's not the point. But, yes, I believe so . . . He left something for you," Oita said.

He walked around to the shipping room and returned with a small packing box.

"Here. Open it."

Eve went to a stool and sat down, untying the string that neatly bound the box. She took out a teacup, one of Oita's, uniform and plain. Slowly she examined the right side, then the left, looking for the blush the way Oita had taught them to look, but the light was dull and flattened out the glaze. She touched the rim, acknowledging its integrity and grace.

"It's one of yours," she said.

"Or yours. Or Ryo-san's."

She stared up at him, startled. His eyes had an impish look.

"I didn't know you kept our work."

"If it's good enough. Look carefully. Can you tell the difference?"

She had already looked. No need to look again. She put it back in the box, as though the knowledge that it might be hers would make it fall apart. Oita turned back to the shelf of jars, leaving her alone with the moment.

"He wished me to convey a message," Oita said, his back still to her. "He said, 'Tell Eve-san that this is all that counts.' "

She sat still, staring down into the open box, controlling the breath that wanted to rush in and out of her lungs.

Oita paid no attention to her, but went about his tasks. This then, or another like it, was what Yamamoto had carried in that night, light-years ago. She could feel once more his hands over hers the instant before she'd snatched them away. Potter's hands. Firm and confident of what they could shape.

She lifted her own hands and looked at them. So ordinary and inadequately considered, with their webs of lines crisscrossing the palms, the clear demarcations at the joints. Nails cut low, cuticles and tips scrubbed clean to a shriveled white. Vessels and veins that stood rigid as snakes when she worked the clay.

"I'm still feeling a little weak," she said finally.

"Don't rush things, Eve-san. You still need rest."

When she reached her room, she opened the trunk and cleared a space for the box in one corner, cushioning it on all sides with camisoles and T-shirts. It seemed odd that the simple act of lifting the lid required so much strength, as if she'd moved a boulder. Perhaps she had, for in her weakened state she had come to see her body as insubstantial, as strange and unexamined as her hands.

What was it that had really frightened her? Not his hands but the dream, she thought, or its strange conclusions. *We are one and the same.* Did the presentation of the cup mean she had learned all that was required of her, that the apprenticeship was over, that now she should go home, and begin again on her own as Ryo-san was now doing? For so long she had thought of herself as the only one outside.

It came to her then, in all its narrowness: her own thin, inflexible shields; the celebration of differences—theirs, not hers; the children reprimanded in her mind, and for what? Throughout the illness, she'd been fed endless cups of water and tea and broth, soothed by the lilt of Obaasan's voice, by Makiko's concerned scold whenever she tried to help. *Not yet, you're still weak.* All of them had hovered and tended and counseled and protected her from all her accustomed urges to get up, get out, move on, as though she were running out of time.

Time. Always time. If only she had seen it before, recognized that it would still be there in a moment, an hour. How available time was here, and not to be hurried. Even Yamamoto, who had seemed so tense, understood this *time.* She had felt it in his hands. It was acceptance that made the understanding. Even the little girls knew this.

She wished she were at the Wadas'. She wanted to sit near the comforting old woman, to let her take her hands as she held the brush and learned the correct sequence of strokes. Kimochi-ii, *Eve-san . . . It takes a long time, and children here start so young.*

Was there time enough left to remove the walls, to tear them down, brick by scorched brick?

★

She was awakened by a moan somewhere in the house, then others jaggedly spaced. She heard shuffling in the hall, the sound of a woman's feet against a hardwood floor. Light seeped in under her door, then Obaasan shushed one of the children.

"We'll have to call a taxi, son."

A man's slippers slapped against heels. Eve wrapped herself in her old robe, once Makiko's, and opened the door. Lights blazed. Little Nanchiko stood inert as a stump in a doorway, sleep filling her eyes. Obaasan spoke to Oita-san in a low voice, but even the children could hear.

"The contractions are still far apart," she said. "There's plenty of time, but she's early. I don't like it."

"Wasn't she early the last time?"

"No, son. She was late."

Eve went to the kitchen and placed the kettle on the fire. She filled the rice cooker, removed pickles from the tub, eggs from the refrigerator. Obaasan came in for a towel.

"I'll feed the children," Eve said.

"Good. Perhaps Oita might have something too."

Makiko screamed, and Obaasan vanished. Eve steeped the tea.

Obaasan darted in again for a fresh compress, her tongue clucking. *Poor Makiko. Everything so complicated when it could be easy. Everything full of pain. But then life is pain. Life is troublesome and full of nuisance, and there was nothing to do.* Skikata ga nai.

A child cried out—Yoko, the baby. Soon to have her own bed. One night with her mother. The next displaced. Put on a child's futon, alone, or perhaps with Obaasan. In the hall, a hurried consultation was taking place.

"What about the children?" Oita asked.

"We can't leave the baby, but Eve-san can look after the girls."

"But—"

"Don't fuss, son. It can't be helped. Eve knows what to do."

Where had it come from, this confidence? She felt amazed, for it had come as easily as a hand lifted into the air.

Eve heard the motor of the village taxi near the house, the soft beep as the car backed up, then the yank and tug of a brake.

Makiko, wrapped in a lightly padded kimono jacket, held on to Obaasan who led her through the house. Oita followed, cradling the baby. Eve watched him from the kitchen door.

He seemed unsure of himself, reduced, lost in a void of authority. He would find himself soon. He must. His shoulders sagged as though worry altered his shape, loosening the solid man of the kiln into a gourd. He would find himself. It was only the stress. It was Makiko's moment, and he had nothing to do.

Eve arranged plates on Obaasan's favorite tray. She used the special plates, the ones reserved for holidays. A treat. A recognition. To celebrate a special rite of passage. *You are such big, important girls now,* she would tell them. *Big enough to be left alone with your father and Auntie Eve.* Alone for several hours, perhaps a day. *Won't it be fun?* They would play their favorite games. She would even take them into Obaasan's garden and look for beetles. *Maybe we'll even send Oto-san out to buy a special cage for our beetles. An insect* danshi, *an apartment house.* Her mind raced with plans.

The car door slammed. Oita spoke to the little girls—a sweet murmurous flow, and then a sniffle at the kitchen door. Nanchiko held her younger sister by the hand.

"Fumi-chan's upset," Nanchiko said. Fumiko looked at Eve solemnly. It wasn't Fumi who was sniffling.

"Look!" Eve said. "Special treats. Okaasan and Obaasan made them for you."

Eve carried the breakfast tray to the table, the little girls trailing after her like lambs. Not a word from either of them, and she feared that any word from her would cause a rush of tears.

She served the rice, milk, walnut treats, pickled eggplants, and bits of fish with their sweet marinade. The girls picked at the pearly kernels; a few tufts entered each mouth. Fumiko moved the walnuts around the tiny round bowl. "Why are we using the New Year's plates?" Nanchiko asked.

As she tried to tell them, the girls put down their bowls and stared into their laps until Nanchiko began to cry. She jumped up from the table and ran out of the room, calling her father.

"Stay right here, Fumi-chan." Eve followed Nanchiko and found her standing in the yard, hands to her face, a soft shaking lump.

Eve knelt beside her and offered her a handkerchief.

"You're not to worry, Nanchiko. Obaasan will telephone and I'll be sure you talk with her. Mother will be back soon."

"Okaasan didn't go away before. The doctor came here."

"Yes, I know. But this time it's different. Better to go to the hospital. Anyway, Obaasan told me that she relied on Nanchiko to look after Fumi-chan."

Nanchiko looked up, the hands parting from the face, a curtain opened.

"It won't be for long. I promise you. Let's go finish our breakfast."

She offered her hand, but the child reached out instead for the long blue tail of Eve's work shirt and clung to it. At the table, Eve disengaged the child's hand and offered her fresh, warm rice. Fumiko hadn't budged. Her rice bowl stood half empty, the walnuts dispersed, the eggplants untouched. Eve leaned over and said, in a whisper, "It's okay. I'll tell Obaasan we ate so much breakfast that we all grew round as tree frogs." The little girls peeped up. "And fat as Badger-chan!" Fumiko smiled.

They followed her into the kitchen and watched as she placed the dishes in the deep stone sink.

"Want to help?"

Immediately they found the dish towels and stood, one on either side of her, receiving each wet dish with a care and dexterity she couldn't remember in herself.

They were like a cavalcade, moving across the landscape of the house, from room to room, through a day without objects. She heard them pattering behind her until she gave them small pick-up put-down chores to keep their hands busy. When the dishes were done, the bedding put away, the clothes picked up, Eve went back to the room where they slept and found the butterfly nets and cage. They took these only because she told them to, tools of no great pleasure.

She grew tense as the morning wore on. She'd expected Obaasan to call, and it was only after she'd followed Nanchiko into the yard that

she realized Oita must have gone with them. Of course! Obaasan
would have the baby. Who would assist Makiko? Eve wondered what
Nanchiko would have done had she realized that Oita was truly gone
from the family compound and not simply hiding in the work building.
She'd seen a child lost on a Kyoto street, and what she had seen was not
just fear and tears. All pins holding the child together had been pulled
out, as if to lose a parent were to lose your mind. She wouldn't tell the
little girls.

She handed Nanchiko the net, Fumiko the beetle cage. Together
they walked out toward the garden. A solitary white cabbage moth
flitted off the plants, but was not pursued.

A cheerleader at a game without fans. There was nothing the
little girls could be induced to try, at least with any conviction. She
had sustained their interest for a precious ten minutes by what
appeared to be a congregation of ladybugs—a sight she herself had
never seen. They counted the swarm of tiny tanks, until this distrac-
tion wore itself out.

Beyond the perimeter of the garden, the meadow beckoned. They
would have a walk, yes! out to the place where Nanchiko had found a
home for her worm. "Come," she said, and they followed behind,
through untamed grass that tickled their legs. She wondered if Fumiko
had ever come here. It seemed unlikely, considering Nanchiko's reaction all those months ago. Their life was so proscribed, bounded by
kitchen and garden, the proximity of Mother and Obaasan, cushioned
by the resilient floor, the *tatami,* the foundation of the universe.

The girls trudged behind her now, without pleasure but without
complaint, to the furthest point of the family property, where Oita dug
his clay. Eve stopped at the edge of it and stooped down, thrusting her
hand into the loosened soil.

"Do you know what this is?" she asked.

Nanchiko nodded. Eve sat on weeds near the edge of the clay pit.
She filled her hand and kneaded until she felt the elasticity coming up.
She rolled the clay between her palms, thinning it into a rope. When it
was thin enough, she coiled it into a circle and pinched the ends together, took another handful, kneading and rolling another length.

"Go ahead," she said.

"We'll get our dresses dirty," said Nanchiko.

"Then I'll wash them for you. Here. Sit on this." She took the large square handkerchief, her *furoshiki,* that she carried everywhere now, and spread it across the grass. It wasn't really big enough, but each sat on one half as if the very fact it was provided was enough to keep them clean.

Eve took a handful of clay, rolled it into a ball, and gave it to Nanchiko, rolling a second ball for Fumiko. They took the clay gingerly. The unfamiliar moment must be weighed and measured, she realized, before giving in. Perhaps the pleasurable possibilities were not there to see, but had to be conferred.

"Go ahead," she said. "Make a snake. Make anything you like."

She took a fresh lump for herself and moved it around and around her hands. She thrust her right thumb into the heart of this ball and pinched, the ball moving in its circumference, the hollow space widening and taking on depth. Nanchiko watched her. Fumiko had already begun to roll out snakes of clay, her small hands rubbing skillfully back and forth. A natural, Eve thought. She should have guessed, and she watched the younger girl with delight, as though she were seeing a child she'd never seen before. Nanchiko began pinching a hollow in her own ball. As they pressed and kneaded and rolled, a strange quietude settled over them. The girls said little, moving their small hands, unconcerned with anything else.

There was time, she thought. There had to be, and still so much to learn. Help would be at a premium, what with Ryo-san gone as well. They would need her for a while longer. All of them. She couldn't possibly leave. Not yet.

Fumiko stacked her ropes of clay into a tall tube. Before Eve could advise her to smooth the surface, inside and out, she did it herself, blending the ridges together into a sweet, uneven bowl. When she was finished, she placed it carefully on the grass beside her.

"I'm tired," she said.

"Me too," said Nanchiko, holding her pinch pot out for Eve to admire.

"So am I," said Eve. "Let's go back. We'll give these to your father."

The girls giggled and came to life, scampered to their feet, straightening the backs of their dresses and wiping flecks of grass from their legs. Her courage sagged. They wouldn't look for Oita, but leave the pots on the kitchen step to dry. Then they would go in and bathe. Surely by that time he would have returned.

"Hold them carefully, now. In both hands."

Eve picked up her small bowl, making sure each girl was cradling her own, then grabbed the *furoshiki* by one end and draped it around her neck. Single file, they took off through the meadow, Fumiko in front, then Nanchiko, Eve bringing up the rear.

"Straight ahead, Fumi-chan . . . That's right. See the trail we made through the grass? . . . A little to your left there. That's fine . . . Don't worry, Nanchiko. Take your time. Think how pleased Oto-san will be . . ."

When they reached the boundary of the garden, she could make out Oita over the top of the foliage, standing near the kitchen door, unable to see their approach.

"Here we are!" Eve called, the little girls echoing.

The girls picked up speed. Eve yelled after them, "Take care of the pots!" Nanchiko laughed and called out to him, "Oto-san! Papa! How is Okaasan? When is she coming back?" Fumiko called out after her, adding something of her own. "I miss Obaasan. Is she here yet?"

The worried slump of Oita's body filled out at the sound of their voices, taking on its familiar, agreeable weight. "Okaasan is going to be fine," he called back. "Everyone's fine. The new baby too."

The girls approached on the run. He spread his arms wide, laughing, placing his hands in pretended amazement against his forehead as his daughters offered up their small clay bowls and everyone talked at once.

Catherine Browder has lived and worked in Japan, Taiwan, and England. She is the author of two prizewinning plays. Her stories have appeared in *American Fiction* (Birch Lane Press), *New Letters, Prairie Schooner, Shenandoah,* and elsewhere. She is the recipient of a Writer's Award from the Missouri Arts Council, the Margot Jones Playwriting Award, the Seaton Award in Fiction from *Kansas Quarterly,* and she was a finalist for the Drue Heinz Literature Prize.

Browder graduated from the University of Michigan in Ann Arbor, where she grew up, and later attended the Iowa Writers' Workshop. She lives with her husband in Kansas City, Missouri, and teaches English as a second language at Don Bosco Center.

The Clay That Breathes was typeset in
Bembo 11/13 by Graphic Arts Services
and printed by Edwards Brothers Incorporated.
The paper is an acid-free Glatfelter Natural.